HANS BRINKER

OR

THE SILVER SKATES
A Story of Life in Holland

BY

MARY MAPES DODGE

The
GOLDSMITH
Publishing Company
CHICAGO ILL.
GP
MADE IN U.S.A.

CONTENTS

CONTENTS

HANS BRINKER

or

The Silver Skates

CHAPTER I

HANS AND GRETEL

ON a bright December morning long ago, two thinly clad children were kneeling upon the bank of a frozen canal in Holland.

The sun had not yet appeared, but the gray sky was parted near the horizon, and its edges shone crimson with the coming day. Most of the good Hollanders were enjoying a placid morning nap; even Mynheer von Stoppelnoze, that worthy old Dutchman, was still slumbering "in beautiful repose."

Now and then some peasant woman, poising a well filled basket upon her head, came skimming over the glassy surface of the canal; or a lusty boy, skating to his day's work in the town, cast a good-natured grimace toward the shivering pair as he flew along.

Meanwhile, with many a vigorous puff and pull, the brother and sister, for such they were, seemed to be fastening something upon their feet—not skates, certainly, but clumsy pieces of wood narrowed and smoothed at their lower edge, and pierced with holes, through which were threaded strings of raw hide.

These queer looking affairs had been made by the boy Hans. His mother was a poor peasant woman, too poor to even think of such a thing as buying skates for her little ones. Rough as these were, they had afforded the children many a happy hour upon the ice; and now as with cold, red fingers our young Hollanders tugged at the strings—their solemn faces bending closely over their knees—no vision of impossible iron runners came to dull the satisfaction flowing within.

In a moment the boy arose, and with a pompous swing of the arms, and a careless "Come on, Gretel," glided easily across the canal.

"Ah, Hans," called his sister plaintively, "this foot is not well yet. The strings hurt me on last Market day; and now I cannot bear them tied in the same place."

"Tie them higher up, then," answered Hans, as without looking at her he performed a wonderful cat's-cradle step on the ice.

"How can I? The string is too short."

Giving vent to a good-natured Dutch whistle, the English of which was that girls were troublesome creatures, he steered towards her.

"You are foolish to wear such shoes, Gretel, when you have a stout leather pair. Your klompen* would be better than these."

"Why, Hans! Do you forget? The father threw my beautiful new shoes in the fire. Before I knew what he had done they were all curled up in the midst of the burning peat. I can skate with these, but not with my wooden ones. Be careful now—"

Hans had taken a string from his pocket. Humming a tune as he knelt beside her, he proceeded to fasten Gretel's skate with all the force of his strong young arm.

"Oh! oh!" she cried, in real pain.

*Wooden shoes.

With an impatient jerk Hans unwound the string. He would have cast it upon the ground in true big-brother style, had he not just then spied a tear trickling down his sister's cheek.

"I'll fix it—never fear," he said, with sudden tenderness, "but we must be quick; the mother will need us soon."

Then he glanced inquiringly about him, first at the ground, next at some bare willow branches above his head, and finally at the sky now gorgeous with streaks of blue, crimson and gold

Finding nothing in any of these localities to meet his need, his eye suddenly brightened as, with the air of a fellow who knew what he was about, he took off his cap and removing the tattered lining, adjusted it in a smooth pad over the top of Gretel's worn-out shoe.

"Now," he cried triumphantly, at the same time arranging the strings as briskly as his benumbed fingers would allow, "can you bear some pulling?"

Gretel drew up her lips as if to say "hurt away," but made no further response.

In another moment they were laughing together, as hand in hand they flew along the canal, never thinking whether the ice would bear or not, for in Holland, ice is generally an all-Winter affair. It settles itself upon the water in a determined kind of way, and so far from growing thin and uncertain every time the sun is a little severe upon it, it gathers its force day by day and flashes defiance to every beam.

Presently, squeak! squeak! sounded something beneath Hans' feet. Next his strokes grew shorter, ending ofttimes with a jerk, and finally, he lay sprawling upon the ice, kicking against the air with many a fantastic flourish.

"Ha! ha!" laughed Gretel, "that was a fine tumble!" But a tender heart was beating under her coarse blue jacket and, even as she laughed, she came, with a graceful sweep, close to her prostrate brother.

"Are you hurt, Hans? oh you are laughing! catch me now"—and she darted away shivering no longer, but with cheeks all aglow, and eyes sparkling with fun.

Hans sprang to his feet and started in brisk pursuit, but it was no easy thing to catch Gretel. Before she had traveled very far, her skates too, began to squeak.

Believing that discretion was the better part of valor she turned suddenly and skated into her pursuer's arms.

"Ha! ha! I've caught you!" cried Hans.

"Ha! ha! I caught you," she retorted, struggling to free herself.

Just then a clear, quick voice was heard calling, "Hans! Gretel!"

"It's the mother," said Hans, looking solemn in an instant.

By this time the canal was gilded with sunlight. The pure morning air was very delightful, and skaters were gradually increasing in numbers. It was hard to obey the summons. But Gretel and Hans were good children; without a thought of yielding to the temptation to linger, they pulled off their skates leaving half the knots still tied. Hans, with his great square shoulders, and bushy yellow hair, towered high above his blue-eyed little sister as they trudged homeward. He was fifteen years old and Gretel was only twelve. He was a solid, heartylooking boy, with honest eyes and a brow that seemed to bear a sign "goodness within" just as

the little Dutch zomerhuis* wears a motto over its
portal. Gretel was lithe and quick; her eyes had a
dancing light in them, and while you looked at her
cheek the color paled and deepened just as it does
upon a bed of pink and white blossoms when the
wind is blowing.

As soon as the children turned from the canal they
could see their parents' cottage. Their mother's tall
form, arrayed in jacket and petticoat and close-fit-
ting cap, stood, like a picture, in the crooked frame
of the doorway. Had the cottage been a mile away,
it would still have seemed near. In that flat country
every object stands out plainly in the distance; the
chickens show as distinctly as the windmills. Indeed, were it not for the dikes and the high banks
of the canals, one could stand almost anywhere in
middle Holland without seeing a mound or a ridge
between the eye and the "jumping-off place."

None had better cause to know the nature of these
same dikes than Dame Brinker and the panting
youngsters now running at her call. But before stat-
ing why, let me ask you to take a rocking-chair trip
with me to that far country where you may see, perhaps for the first time, some curious things that
Hans and Gretel saw every day.

*Summer-house.

CHAPTER II

HOLLAND

Holland is one of the queerest countries under the sun. It should be called Odd-land or Contrary-land, for in nearly everything it is different from other parts of the world. In the first place, a large portion of the country is lower than the level of the sea. Great dikes or bulwarks have been erected at a heavy cost of money and labor, to keep the ocean where it belongs. On certain parts of the coast it sometimes leans with all its weight against the land, and it is as much as the poor country can do to stand the pressure. Sometimes the dikes give way, or spring a leak, and the most disastrous results ensue. They are high and wide, and the tops of some of them are covered with buildings and trees. They have even fine public roads upon them, from which horses may look down upon way-side cottages. Often the keels of floating ships are higher than the roofs of the dwellings. The stork clattering to her young on the house-peak may feel that her nest is lifted far out of danger, but the croaking frog in neighboring bulrushes is nearer the stars than she. Water-bugs dart backward and forward above the heads of the chimney swallows; and willow trees seem drooping with shame, because they cannot reach as high as the reeds near by.

Ditches, canals, ponds, rivers and lakes are everywhere to be seen. High, but not dry, they shine in the sunlight, catching nearly all the bustle and the business, quite scorning the tame fields stretching damply beside them. One is tempted to ask, "Which is Holland—the shores or the water?" The very verdure that should be confined to the land has made a mistake and settled upon the fishponds. In fact the entire country is a kind of saturated sponge, or, as the English poet, Butler, called it,

"A land that rides at anchor, and is moor'd,
In which they do not live, but go aboard."

Persons are born, live and die, and even have their gardens on canal-boats. Farm-houses, with roofs like great slouched hats pulled over their eyes, stand on wooden legs with a tucked-up sort of air, as if to say "we intend to keep dry if we can." Even the horses wear a wide stool on each hoof to lift them out of the mire. In short, the landscape everywhere suggests a paradise for ducks. It is a glorious country in summer for bare-footed girls and boys. Such wadings! such mimic ship sailing! Such rowing, fishing and swimming! Only think of a chain of puddles where one can launch chip boats all day long, and never set all young America rushing in a body toward the Zuider Zee.

Dutch cities seem at first to be a bewildering jungle of houses, bridges, churches and ships, sprouting into masts, steeples and trees. In some cities vessels are hitched like horses, to their owners' doorposts and receive their freight from the upper windows. Mothers scream to Lodewyk and Kassy not to swing on the garden gate for fear they may be drowned! Water-roads are more frequent there than common roads and railways; water-fences in the form of lazy green ditches enclose pleasure-ground, polder and garden.

Sometimes fine green hedges are seen; but wooden fences such as we have in America are rarely met with in Holland. As for stone fences, a Dutchman would lift his hands with astonishment at the very idea. There is no stone there, excepting those great

masses of rock, that have been brought from other
lands to strengthen and protect the coast. All the
small stones or pebbles, if there ever were any, seem
to be imprisoned in pavements or quite melted away.
Boys with strong, quick arms may grow from pina-
fores to full beards without ever finding one to start
the water-rings or set the rabbits flying. The water-
roads are nothing less than canals intersecting the
country in every direction. These are of all sizes,
from the great North Holland Ship Canal, which is
the wonder of the world, to those which a boy can
leap. Water-omnibuses, called *trekschuiten**, constantly ply up and down these roads for the convey-
ance of passengers; and water drays, called *pak-
schuyten**, are used for carrying fuel and merchandise. Instead of green country lanes, green canals
stretch from field to barn and from barn to garden;
and the farms or *polders,* as they are termed, are
merely great lakes pumped dry. Some of the bus-
iest streets are water, while many of the country
roads are paved with brick. The city boats with
their round sterns, gilded prows and gaily painted
sides, are unlike any others under the sun; and a
Dutch wagon with its funny little crooked pole, is
a perfect mystery of mysteries.

"One thing is clear," cries Master Brightside, "the
inhabitants need never be thirsty." But no, Odd-
land is true to itself still. Notwithstanding the sea
pushing to get in, and the lakes struggling to get
out, and the overflowing canals, rivers and ditches,
in many districts there is no water fit to swallow;
our poor Hollanders must go dry, or drink wine and
beer, or send far into the inland to Utrecht, and

*Canal boats. Some of the first named are over thirty feet
long. They look like green houses lodged on barges, and are
drawn by horses walking along the bank of the canal.

other favored localities, for that precious fluid older
than Adam yet young as the morning dew. Sometimes, indeed, the inhabitants can swallow a shower
when they are provided with any means of catching
it; but generally they are like the Albatross-haunted
sailors in Coleridge's famous poem of "The Ancient
Mariner"—they see

> "Water, water everywhere,
> Nor any drop to drink!"

Great flapping windmills all over the country make
it look as if flocks of huge sea-birds were just settling. Everywhere one sees the funniest trees, bobbed
into fantastical shapes, with their trunks painted a
dazzling white, yellow or red. Horses are often
yoked three abreast. Men, women and children go
clattering about in wooden shoes with loose heels;
peasant girls who cannot get beaux for love, hire
them for money to escort them to the Kermis*; and
husbands and wives lovingly harness themselves side
by side on the bank of the canal and drag their pak-
schuyts to market.

Another peculiar feature of Holland is the dune or
sand-hill. These are numerous along certain portions of the coast. Before they were sown with
coarse reed-grass and other plants, to hold them
down, they used to send great storms of sand over
the inland. So, to add to the oddities, farmers sometimes dig down under the surface to find their soil,
and on windy days dry showers of sand often fall
upon fields that have grown wet under a week of
sunshine.

In short, almost the only familiar thing we Yank-
ees can meet with in Holland is a harvest-song which
is quite popular there, though no linguist could trans-

*Fair.

late it. Even then we must shut our eyes and listen
only to the tune which I leave you to guess.

> "Yanker didee dudel down
> Didee dudel lawnter;
> Yankee viver, voover, vown,
> Botermelk und Tawnter!"

On the other hand, many of the oddities of Holland serve only to prove the thrift and perseverance
of the people. There is not a richer, or more carefully tilled garden-spot in the whole world than this
leaky, springy little country. There is not a braver,
more heroic race than its quiet passive-looking inhabitants. Few nations have equaled it in important discoveries and inventions; none has excelled
it in commerce, navigation, learning and science,—
or set as noble examples in the promotion of educa-
tion and public charities; and none in proportion to
its extent has expended more money and labor upon
public works.

Holland has its shining annals of noble and illus-
trious men and women; its grand, historic records
of patience, resistance and victory; its religious freedom, its enlightened enterprise, its art, its music
and its literature. It has truly been called "the
battle field of Europe," as truly may we consider it
the Asylum of the world, for the oppressed of every
nation have there found shelter and encouragement.
If we Americans, who, after all, are homeopathic
preparations of Holland stock, can laugh at the
Dutch, and call them human beavers, and hint that
their country may float off any day at high tide, we
can also feel proud, and say they have proved
themselves heroes, and that their country will not
float off while there is a Dutchman left to grapple it.

There are said to be at least ninety-nine hundred
large windmills in Holland, with sails ranging from

eighty to one hundred and twenty feet long. They are employed in sawing timber, beating hemp, grinding, and many other kinds of work; but their principal use is for pumping water from the lowlands into the canals, and for guarding against the inland freshets that so often deluge the country. Their yearly cost is said to be nearly ten millions of dollars. The large ones are of great power. Their huge, circular tower, rising sometimes from the midst of factory buildings is surmounted with a smaller one tapering into a cap-like roof. This upper tower is encircled at its base with a balcony, high above which juts the axis turned by its four prodigious, ladder-backed sails.

Many of the windmills are primitive affairs, seeming sadly in need of Yankee "improvements;" but some of the new ones are admirable. They are so constructed that, by some ingenious contrivance, they present their fans, or wings, to the wind in precisely the right direction to work with the requisite power. In other words, the miller may take a nap and feel quite sure that his mill will study the wind, and make the most of it, until he wakens. Should there be but a slight current of air every sail will spread itself to catch the faintest breath; but if a heavy "blow" should come, they will shrink at its touch, like great mimosa leaves, and only give it half a chance to move them.

One of the old prisons of Amsterdam, called the Rasphouse, because the thieves and vagrants who were confined there were employed in rasping logwood, had a cell for the punishment of lazy prisoners. In one corner of this cell was a pump and, in another, an opening through which a steady stream of water was admitted. The prisoner could take his choice, either to stand still and be drowned,

or to work for dear life at the pump and keep the
flood down until his jailer chose to relieve him. Now
it seems to me that, throughout Holland, Nature
has introduced this little diversion on a grand scale.
The Dutch have always been forced to pump for
their very existence and probably must continue to
do so to the end of time.

Every year millions of dollars are spent in re-
pairing dikes, and regulating water levels. If these
important duties were neglected the country would
be uninhabitable. Already, dreadful consequences,
as I have said, have followed the bursting of these
dikes. Hundreds of villages and towns have from
time to time been buried beneath the rush of waters,
and nearly a million of persons have been destroyed.
One of the most fearful inundations ever known occurred in the autumn of the year 1570. Twenty-
eight terrible floods had before that time overwhelm-
ed portions of Holland, but this was the most terrible of all. The unhappy country had long been
suffering under Spanish tyranny, now, it seemed, the
crowning point was given to its troubles. When we
read Motley's history of the Rise of the Dutch Re-
public we learn to revere the brave people who have
endured, suffered and dared so much.

Mr. Motley in his thrilling account of the great
inundation tells us how a long continued and violent
gale had been sweeping the Atlantic waters into the
North Sea, piling them against the coasts of the
Dutch provinces; how the dikes, tasked beyond their
strength, burst in all directions; how even the Hand-
bos, a bulwark formed of oaken piles, braced with
iron, moored with heavy anchors and secured by
gravel and granite, was snapped to pieces like pack-
thread; how fishing boats and bulky vessels floating
up into the country became entangled among the

trees, or beat in the roofs and walls of dwellings, and how at last all Friesland was converted into an angry sea. "Multitudes of men, women, children, of horses, oxen, sheep, and every domestic animal, were struggling in the waves in every direction. Every boat and every article which could serve as a boat were eagerly seized upon. Every house was inundated, even the grave-yards gave up their dead. The living infant in his cradle, and the long-buried corpse in his coffin, floated side by side. The ancient flood seemed about to be renewed. Everywhere, up-on the tops of trees, upon the steeples of churches, human beings were clustered, praying to God for mercy, and to their fellowmen for assistance. As the storm at last was subsiding, boats began to ply in every direction, saving those who were struggling in the water, picking fugitives from roofs and tree tops, and collecting the bodies of those already drowned." No less than one hundred thousand hu-man beings had perished in a few hours. Thousands upon thousands of dumb creatures lay dead upon the waters; and the damage done to property of every description was beyond calculation.

Robles, the Spanish Governor, was foremost in noble efforts to save life and lessen the horrors of the catastrophe. He had formerly been hated by the Dutch because of his Spanish or Portuguese blood, but by his goodness and activity in their hour of dis-aster, he won all hearts to gratitude. He soon intro-duced an improved method of constructing the dikes, and passed a law that they should in future be kept up by the owners of the soil. There were fewer heavy floods from this time, though within less than three hundred years six fearful inundations swept over the land.

In the Spring there is always great danger of inland freshets, especially in times of thaw, because the rivers, choked with blocks of ice, overflow before they can discharge their rapidly rising waters into the ocean. Added to this, the sea chafing and pressing against the dikes, it is no wonder that Holland is often in a state of alarm. The greatest care is taken to prevent accidents. Engineers and workmen are stationed all along in threatened places and a close watch is kept up night and day. When a general signal of danger is given, the inhabitants all rush to the rescue, eager to combine against their common foe. As everywhere else, straw is supposed to be of all things the most helpless in the water, of course in Holland it must be rendered the main stay against a rushing tide. Huge straw mats are pressed against the embankments, fortified with clay and heavy stone, and once adjusted, the ocean dashes against them in vain.

Raff Brinker, the father of Gretel and Hans, had for years been employed upon the dikes. It was at the time of a threatened inundation, when in the midst of a terrible storm, in darkness and sleet, the men were laboring at a weak spot near the Veermyk sluice, that he fell from the scaffolding, and was taken home insensible. From that hour he never worked again; though he lived on, mind and memory were gone.

Gretel could not remember him otherwise than as the strange, silent man, whose eyes followed her vacantly whichever way she turned; but Hans had recollections of a hearty, cheerful-voiced father who was never tired of bearing him upon his shoulder, and whose careless song still seemed echoing near when he lay awake at night and listened.

CHAPTER III

THE SILVER SKATES

Dame Brinker earned a scanty support for her family by raising vegetables, spinning and knitting. Once she had worked on board the barges plying up and down the canal, and had occasionally been harnessed with other women to the towing rope of a pakschuyt plying between Broak and Amsterdam. But when Hans had grown strong and large, he had insisted upon doing all such drudgery in her place. Besides, her husband had become so very helpless of late, that he required her constant care. Although not having as much intelligence as a little child, he was yet strong of arm and very hearty, and Dame Brinker had sometimes great trouble in controlling him.

"Ah, children, he was so good and steady," she would sometimes say, "and as wise as a lawyer. Even the Burgomaster would stop to ask him a question, and now alack! he don't know his wife and little ones. You remember the father, Hans, when he was himself—a great brave man—don't you?"

"Yes, indeed, mother, he knew everything, and could do anything under the sun—and how he would sing! why, you used to laugh and say it was enough to set the windmills dancing."

"So I did. Bless me! how the boy remembers! Gretel, child, take that knitting needle from your father, quick; he'll get it in his eyes maybe; and put the shoe on him. His poor feet are like ice half the time, but I can't keep 'em covered all I can do—" and then half wailing, half humming, Dame Brinker would sit down, and fill the low cottage with the whirr of her spinning wheel.

Nearly all the out-door work, as well as the house-hold labor, was performed by Hans and Gretel. At certain seasons of the year the children went out day after day to gather peat, which they would stow away in square, brick-like pieces, for fuel. At other times, when home-work permitted, Hans rode the towing-horses on the canals, earning a few stivers* a day; and Gretel tended geese for the neighboring farmers.

Hans was clever at carving in wood, and both he and Gretel were good gardeners. Gretel could sing and sew and run on great, high, home-made stilts better than any girl for miles around . She could learn a ballad in five minutes, and find, in its season, any weed or flower you could name; but she dreaded books, and often the very sight of the figuring-board in the old school-house would set her eyes swimming. Hans, on the contrary, was slow and steady. The harder the task, whether in study or daily labor, the better he liked it. Boys who sneered at him out of school, on account of his patched clothes and scant leather breeches, were forced to yield him the post of honor in nearly every class. It was not long be-fore he was the only youngster in the school who had not stood at least once in the corner of horrors, where hung a dreaded whip, and over it this motto:

*Leer, leer! jou luigaart, of dit endje tuow zal je leeren!"

It was only in winter that Gretel and Hans could be spared to attend school; and for the past month they had been kept at home because their mother needed their services. Raff Brinker required con-stant attention, and there was black bread to be made, and the house to be kept clean, the stockings

*A stiver is worth about two cents of our money.
*(Learn! Learn! you idler, or this rope's end shall teach you.)

and other things to be knitted and sold in the market place.

While they were busily assisting their mother on this cold December morning, a merry troop of girls and boys came skimming down the canal. There were fine skaters among them, and as the bright medley of costumes flitted by, it looked from a distance as though the ice had suddenly thawed, and some gay tulip-bed were floating along on the current.

There was the rich burgomaster's daughter, Hilda van Gleck, with her costly furs and loose-fitting velvet sacque; and, near by, a pretty peasant girl, Annie Bouman, jauntily attired in a coarse scarlet jacket and a blue skirt just short enough to display the gray homespun hose to advantage. Then there was the proud Rychie Korbes, whose father, Mynheer van Korbes, was one of the leading men of Amsterdam; and, flocking closely around her, Carl Schummel, Peter and Ludwig van Holp, Jacob Poot, and a very small boy rejoicing in the tremendous name of Voostenwalbert Schimmelpenninck. There were nearly twenty other boys and girls in the party, and one and all seemed full of excitement and frolic.

Up and down the canal, within the space of a half mile they skated, exerting their racing powers to the utmost. Often the swiftest among them was seen to dodge from under the very nose of some pompous law-giver, or doctor, who with folded arms was skating leisurely toward the town; or a chain of girls would suddenly break at the approach of a fat old burgomaster who, with gold-headed cane poised in the air, was puffing his way to Amsterdam. Equipped in skates wonderful to behold, from their superb strappings, and dazzling runners curving over the instep and topped with gilt balls, he would

open his fat eyes a little if one of the maidens chanced to drop him a curtsy, but would not dare to bow
in return for fear of losing his balance.

Not only pleasure-seekers and stately men of note
were upon the canal.   There were work-people, with
weary eyes, hastening to their shops and factories;
market-women with loads upon their heads; ped-
dlers bending with their packs; barge-men with
shaggy hair and bleared faces, jostling roughly on
their way; kind-eyed clergymen speeding perhaps to
the bedsides of the dying; and, after a while, groups,
of children, with satchels slung over their shoulders,
whizzing past, towards the distant school.   One and
all wore skates, excepting, indeed, a muffled-up
farmer whose queer cart bumped along on the margin of the canal.

Before long our merry boys and girls were almost
lost in the confusion of bright colors, the ceaseless
motion, and the gleaming of skates flashing back the
sunlight.   We might have known no more of them
had not the whole party suddenly come to a stand-
still, and grouping themselves out of the way of the
passers-by, all talked at once to a pretty little
maiden, whom they had drawn from the tide of people flowing toward the town.

"Oh, Katrinka!" they cried, in a breath, "have you
heard of it?   The race—we want you to join us!"

"What race?" asked Katrinka, laughing—"Don't
all talk at once, please, I can't understand!"

Every one panted and looked at Rychie Korbes,
who was their acknowledged spokeswoman.

"Why," said Rychie, "we are to have a grand skating match on the twentieth, on *Mevrouw van
Gleck's birthday.   It's all Hilda's work.   They are
going to give a splendid prize to the best skater."

*Mrs. or Madame (pronounced Meffrow).

"Yes," chimed in a half-a-dozen voices, "a beautiful pair of silver skates—perfectly magnificent! with, oh! such straps and silver bells and buckles!"

"Who said they had bells?" put in the small voice of the boy with the big name.

"I say so, Master Voost," replied Rychie.

"So they have—" "No I'm sure they haven't—" "Oh, how can you say so—" "It's an arrow—" "And Mynheer van Korbes told my mother they had bells —"same from sundry of the excited group; but Mynheer Voostenwalbert Schimmelpenninck essayed to settle the matter with a decisive—

"Well, you don't any of you know a single thing about it; they haven't a sign of a bell on them, they —"

"Oh! oh!" and the chorus of conflicting opinion broke forth again.

"The girls' pair are to have bells," interposed Hilda, quietly, "but there is to be another pair for the boys with an arrow engraved upon the sides."

"There! I told you so!" cried nearly all the youngsters in a breath.

Katrinka looked at them with bewildered eyes.

"Who is to try?" she asked.

"All of us," answered Rychie. "It will be such fun! And you must, too, Katrinka. But it's school time now, we will talk it all over at noon. Oh! you will join of course."

Kartinka, without replying, made a graceful pirouette, and laughing out a coquettish—"Don't you hear the last bell? Catch me!"—darted off toward the school-house, standing half a mile away, on the canal.

All started, pell-mell, at this challenge, but they tried in vain to catch the bright-eyed, laughing creature who, with golden hair streaming in the sunlight, cast back many a sparkling glance of triumph as she floated onward.

Beautiful Katrinka! Flushed with youth and health, all life and mirth and motion, what wonder thine image, ever floating in advance, sped through one boy's dreams that night! What wonder that it seemed his darkest hour when, years afterward, thy presence floated away from him forever.

CHAPTER IV

HANS AND GRETEL FIND A FRIEND

At noon our young friends poured forth from the school-house intent upon having an hour's practicing upon the canal.

They had skated but a few moments when Carl Schummel said mockingly to Hilda:

"There's a pretty pair just coming upon the ice! The little rag-pickers! Their skates must have been a present from the king direct."

"They are patient creatures," said Hilda gently. "It must have been hard to learn to skate upon such queer affairs. They are very poor peasants, you see. The boy has probably made the skates himself."

Carl was somewhat abashed.

"Patient they may be, but as for skating, they start off pretty well only to finish with a jerk. They could move well to your new staccato piece I think."

Hilda laughed pleasantly and left him. After joining a small detachment of the racers, and sailing past every one of them, she halted beside Gretel who, with eager eyes, had been watching the sport.

"What is your name, little girl?"

"Gretel, my lady," answered the child, somewhat awed by Hilda's rank, though they were nearly of the same age, "and my brother is called Hans."

"Hans is a stout fellow," said Hilda, cheerily, "and seems to have a warm stove somewhere within him, but you look cold. You should wear more clothing, little one."

Gretel, who had nothing else to wear, tried to laugh as she answered:

"I am not so very little. I am past twelve years old."

"Oh, I beg your pardon. You see I am nearly fourteen, and so large for my age that other girls seem small to me, but that is nothing. Perhaps you will shoot up far above me yet; not unless you dress more warmly, though—shivering girls never grow."

Hans flushed as he saw tears rising in Gretel's eyes.

"My sister has not complained of the cold; but this is bitter weather they say—" and he looked sadly upon Gretel.

"It is nothing," said Gretel. "I am often warm— too warm when I am skating. You are good, jufvrouw,* to think of it."

"No, no," answered Hilda, quite angry at herself. "I am careless, cruel; but I meant no harm. I wanted to ask you—I mean—if—" and here Hilda, coming to the point of her errand, faltered before the poorly clad but noble-looking children she wished to serve.

"What is it, young lady?" exclaimed Hans eagerly. "If there is any service I can do—any—"

"Oh! no, no," laughed Hilda, shaking off her embarrassment, "I only wished to speak to you about the grand race. Why do you not join it? You both can skate well, and the ranks are free. Any one may enter for the prize."

Gretel looked wistfully at Hans, who tugging at his cap, answered respectfully:

"Ah, jufrow, even if we could enter, we could skate only a few strokes with the rest. Our skates are hard wood, you see" holding up the sole of his foot, "but they soon become damp, and then they stick and trip us."

*Miss—Young lady (pronounced Yuffrow). In studied or polite address it would be jonvrowe (pronounced Youngfrow).

Gretel's eyes twinkled with fun as she thought of Hans' mishap in the morning, but she blushed as she faltered out timidly:

"Oh no, we can't join; but may we be there, my lady, on the great day to look on?"

"Certainly," answered Hilda, looking kindly into the two earnest faces, and wishing from her heart that she had not spent so much of her monthly allowance for lace and finery. She had but eight kwartjes* left, and they would buy but one pair of skates, at the furthest.

Looking down with a sigh at the two pair of feet so very different in size, she asked:

"Which is of you is the better skater?"

"Gretel," replied Hans promptly.

"Hans," answered Gretel, in the same breath.

Hilda smiled.

"I cannot buy you each a pair of skates, or even one good pair; but here are eight kwartjes. Decide between you which stands the best chance of winning the race, and buy the skates accordingly. I wish I had enough to buy better ones—good-bye!" and, with a nod and a smile, Hilda, after handing the money to the electrified Hans, glided swiftly away to rejoin her companions.

"Jufvrouw! jufvrouw von Gleck!" called Hans in a loud tone, stumbling after her as well as he could, for one of his skate-strings was untied.

Hilda turned, and with one hand raised to shield her eyes from the sun, seemed to him to be floating through the air, nearer and nearer.

"We cannot take this money," panted Hans, "though we know your goodness in giving it."

"Why not, indeed?" asked Hilda, flushing.

*A kwartje is a small silver coin worth ten cents in American currency.

"Because," replied Hans, bowing like a clown, but looking with the eye of a prince at the queenly girl "we have not earned it."

Hilda was quick-witted. She had noticed a pretty wooden chain upon Gretel's neck—

"Carve me a chain, Hans, like the one your sister wears."

"That I will, lady, with all my heart, we have whitewood in the house, fine as ivory; you shall have one to-morrow," and Hans tried to return the money.

"No, no," said Hilda decidedly. "That sum will be but a poor price for the chain," and off she darted, outstripping the fleetest among the skaters.

Hans sent a long, bewildered gaze after her; it was useless, he felt, to make any further resistance.

"It is right," he muttered, half to himself, half to his faithful shadow, Gretel, "I must work hard every minute, and sit up half the night if the mother will let me burn a candle; but the chain shall be finished. We may keep the money, Gretel."

"What a good little lady!" cried Gretel clapping her hands with delight, "oh! Hans, was it for nothing the stork settled on our roof last summer? Do you remember how the mother said it would bring us luck, and how she cried when Janzoon Kolp shot him? And she said it would bring him trouble. But the luck has come to us at last! Now, Hans, if mother sends us to town to-morrow you can buy the skates in the market-place."

Hans shook his head. "The young lady would have given us the money to buy skates; but if I earn it, Gretel, it shall be spent for wool. You must have a warm jacket."

"Oh!" cried Gretel, in real dismay, "not buy the skates! Why I am not often cold! Mother says the

blood runs up and down in poor children's veins
humming 'I must keep 'em warm! I must keep 'em
warm'."

"Oh, Hans," she continued with something like a
sob, "don't say you won't buy the skates, it makes me
feel just like crying—besides, I want to be cold—I
mean I'm real, awful warm—so now!"

Hans looked up hurriedly. He had a true Dutch
horrors of tears, or emotion of any kind, and most of
all, he dreaded to see his sister's blue eyes overflowing.

"Now mind," cried Gretel, seeing her advantage,
"I'll feel awful if you give up the skates. I don't
want them, I'm not such a stingy as that; but I want
you to have them, and then when I get bigger they'll
do for me—oh-h—count the pieces, Hans. Did ever
you see so many!"

Hans turned the money thoughtfully in his palm.
Never in all his life had he longed so intensely for a
pair of skates, for he had known of the race and had,
boy-like, fairly ached for a chance to test his powers
with the other children. He felt confident that with
a good pair of steel runners, he could readily distance most of the boys on the canal. Then, too,
Gretel's argument was so plausible. On the other
hand, he knew that she, with her strong but lithe
little frame, needed but a week's practice on good
runners to make her a better skater than Rychie
Korbes or even Katrinka Flack. As soon as this last
thought flashed upon him his resolve was made. If
Gretel would not have the jacket, she should have
the skates.

"No, Gretel," he answered at last, "I can wait.
Some day I may have money enough saved to buy a
fine pair. You shall have these."

Gretel's eyes sparkled; but in another instant she insisted, rather faintly:

"The young lady gave the money to you, Hans. I'd be real bad to take it."

Hans shook his head, resolutely, as he trudged on, causing his sister to half skip and half walk in her effort to keep beside him; by this time they had taken off their wooden "rockers," and were hastening home to tell their mother the good news.

"Oh, I know!" cried Gretel, in a sprightly tone, "you can do this. You can get a pair a little too small for you, and too big for me, and we can take turns and use them. Won't that be fine?" and Gretel clapped her hands again.

Poor Hans! This was a strong temptation, but he pushed it away from him, brave-hearted fellow that he was.

"Nonsense, Gretel. You could never get on with a big pair. You stumbled about with these, like a blind chicken, before I curved off the ends. No, you must have a pair to fit exactly, and you must practice every chance you can get, until the Twentieth comes. My little Gretel shall win the silver skates."

Gretel could not help laughing with delight at the very idea.

"Hans! Gretel!" called out a familiar voice.

"Coming, mother!" and they hastened toward the cottage, Hans still shaking the pieces of silver in his hand.

On the following day, there was not a prouder nor a happier boy in all Holland than Hans Brinker, as he watched his sister, with many a dexterous sweep, flying in and out among the skaters who at sundown thronged the canal. A warm jacket had been given her by the kind-hearted Hilda, and the burst-out shoes had been cobbled into decency by Dame

Brinker. As the little creature darted backward and forward, flushed with enjoyment, and quite unconscious of the many wondering glances bent upon her, she felt that the shining runners beneath her feet had suddenly turned the earth into Fairyland, while "Hans, dear good Hans!" echoed itself over and over again in her grateful heart.

"By den donder!" exclaimed Peter van Holp to Carl Schummel, "but that little one in the red jacket and patched petticoat skates well. Gunst! she has toes on her heels, and eyes in the back of her head! See her! It will be a joke if she gets in the race and beats Katrinka Flack, after all."

"Hush! not so loud!" returned Carl, rather sneeringly. "That little lady in rags is the special pet of Hilda van Gleck. Those shining skates are her gift, if I make no mistake."

"So! so!" exclaimed Peter, with a radiant smile, for Hilda was his best friend. "She has been at her good work there, too!" And Mynheer van Holp, after cutting a double 8 on the ice, to say nothing of a huge P, then a jump, and an H, glided onward until he found himself beside Hilda.

Hand in hand, they skated together, laughingly at first, than staidly talking in a low tone.

Strange to say, Peter van Holp soon arrived at a sudden conviction that his little sister needed a wooden chain just like Hilda's.

Two days afterwards, on St. Nicholas' Eve, Hans, having burned three candle-ends, and cut his thumb into the bargain, stood in the market-place at Amsterdam, buying another pair of skates.

CHAPTER V

SHADOWS IN THE HOME

Good Dame Brinker! As soon as the scanty dinner had been cleared away that noon, she had arrayed herself in her holiday attire, in honor of Saint Nicholas. "It will brighten the children," she thought to herself, and she was not mistaken. This festival dress had been worn very seldom during the past ten years; before that time it had done good service, and had flourished at many a dance and Kermis, when she was known, far and wide, as the pretty Meitje Klenck. The children had sometimes been granted rare glimpses of it as it lay in state in the old oaken chest. Faded and threadbare as it was, it was gorgeous in their eyes, with its white linen tucker, now gathered to her plump throat, and vanishing beneath the trim bodice of blue homespun, and its reddish brown skirt bordered with black. The knitted woolen mitts, and the dainty cap showing her hair, which generally was hidden, made her seem almost like a princess to Gretel, while master Hans grew staid and well-behaved as he gazed.

Soon the little maid, while braiding her own golden tresses, fairly danced around her mother in an ecstasy of admiration.

"Oh, mother, mother, mother, how pretty you are! Look, Hans! isn't it just like a picture?"

"Just like a picture," assented Hans, cheerfully, "just like a picture—only I don't like those stocking things on the hands."

"Not like the mitts, brother Hans! why they're very important—see—they cover up all the red. Oh, mother, how white your arm is where the mitt leaves off, whiter than mine, oh, ever so much whiter. I

declare, mother, the bodice is tight for you. You're
growing! you're surely growing!"

Dame Brinker laughed.

"This was made long ago, lovely, when I wasn't
much thicker about the waist than a churn-dasher.
And how do you like the cap?" turning her head
from side to side.

"Oh, ever so much, mother. It's b-e-a-u-tiful! see!
The father is looking!"

Was the father looking? Alas, only with a dull
stare. His vrouw turned toward him with a start,
something like a blush rising to her cheeks, a questioning sparkle in her eye— The bright look died
away in an instant.

"No, no," she sighed, "he sees nothing. Come,
Hans," (and the smile crept faintly back again,
"don't stand gaping at me all day, and the new skates
waiting for you at Amsterdam."

"Ah, mother," he answered, "you need many
things. Why should I buy skates?"

"Nonsense, child. The money was given to you
on purpose, or the work was—it's all the same thing
—go while the sun is high."

"Yes, and hurry back, Hans!" laughed Gretel,
"we'll race on the canal to-night, if the mother lets
us."

At the very threshold he turned to say—"Your
spinning wheel wants a new treadle, mother."

"You can make it, Hans."

"So I can. That will take no money. But you
need feathers, and wool and meal, and—"

"There, there! That will do. Your silver cannot
buy everything. Ah! Hans, if our stolen money
would but come back on this bright Saint Nicholas
Eve, how glad we would be! Only last night I pray-
ed to the good Saint—"

"Mother!" interrupted Hans in dismay.

"Why not, Hans! Shame on you to reproach me for that! I'm as true a protestant, in sooth, as any fine lady that walks into church, but it's no wrong to turn sometimes to the good Saint Nicholas. Tut! It's a likely story if one can't do that, without one's children flaring up at it—and he the boys' and girls' own saint—hoot! mayhap the colt is a steadier horse than the mare?"

Hans knew his mother too well to offer a word in opposition, when her voice quickened and sharpened as it did (it was often sharp and quick when she spoke of the missing money) so he said gently:

"And what did you ask of good Saint Nicholas, mother?"

"Why to never give the thieves a wink of sleep till they brought it back, to be sure, if he's power to do such things, or else to brighten our wits that we might find it ourselves. Not a sight have I had of it since the day before the dear father was hurt—as you well know, Hans."

"That I do, mother," he answered sadly, "though you have almost pulled down the cottage in searching."

"Aye; but it was of no use," moaned the dame. "'Hiders make best finders'."

Hans started. "Do you think the father could tell aught?" he asked mysteriously.

"Aye, indeed," said Dame Brinker, nodding her head, "I think so, but that is no sign. I never hold the same belief in the matter two days. Mayhap the father paid it off for the great silver watch we have been guarding since that day. But, no—I'll never believe it."

"The watch was not worth a quarter of the money, mother."

"No, indeed; and your father was a shrewd man up to the last moment. He was too steady and thrifty for silly doings."

"Where did the watch come from, I wonder," muttered Hans, half to himself.

Dame Brinker shook her head, and looked sadly toward her husband, who sat staring blankly at the floor. Gretel stood near him, knitting.

"That we shall never know, Hans. I have shown it to the father many a time, but he does not know it from a potato. When he came in that dreadful night to supper, he handed the watch to me and told me to take good care of it until he asked for it again. Just as he opened his lips to say more, Broom Klatterboost came flying in with word that the dike was in danger. Ah! the waters were terrible that holy Pinxter-week! My man, alack, caught up his tools and ran out. That was the last I ever saw of him in his right mind. He was brought in again by midnight, nearly dead, with his poor head all bruised and cut. The fever passed off in time, but never the dullness—that grew worse every day. We shall never know."

Hans had heard all this before. More than once he had seen his mother, in hours of sore need, take the watch from its hiding place, half-resolved to sell it, but she had always conquered the temptation.

"No Hans," she would say, "we must be nearer starving than this before we turn faithless to the father!"

A memory of some such scene crossed her son's mind now; for, after giving a heavy sigh, and filliping a crumb of wax at Gretel across the table, he said:

"Aye, mother, you have done bravely to keep it—

many a one would have tossed it off for gold long
ago."

"And more shame for them!" exclaimed the dame,
indignantly, "I would not do it. Besides, the gentry
are so hard on us poor folks that if they saw such a
thing in our hands, even if we told all, they might
suspect the father of—"

"They would not dare to say such a thing, mother!
If they did—I'd—"

He clenched his fist, and seemed to think that the
rest of his sentence was too terrible to utter in her
presence.

Dame Brinker smiled proudly through her tears
at his interruption.

"Ah, Hans, thou'rt a true, brave lad. We will
never part company with the watch. In his dying
hour the dear father might wake and ask for it."

"Might wake, mother!" echoed Hans, "wake—and
know us?"

"Aye, child," almost whispered his mother, "such
things have been."

By this time Hans had nearly forgotten his proposed errand to Amsterdam. His mother had seldom spoken so familiarly with him. He felt himself
now to be not only her son, but her friend, her ad-
viser.

"You are right, mother. We must never give up
the watch. For the father's sake, we will guard it
always. The money, though, may come to light when
we least expect it."

"Never!" cried Dame Brinker, taking the last
stitch from her needle with a jerk, and laying the
unfinished knitting heavily upon her lap. "There is
no chance! One thousand guilders! and all gone in
a day! One thousand guilders—oh! what ever did

become of them? If they went in an evil way, the
thief would have confessed by this on his dying bed
—he would not dare to die with such guilt on his
soul!"

"He may not be dead yet," said Hans," soothingly.
"any day we may hear of him."

"Ah, child," she said in a changed tone, "what
thief would ever have come here? It was always
neat and clean thank God! but not fine; for the
father and I saved and saved that we might have
something laid by. 'Little and often soon fills the
pouch.' We found it so, in truth; besides, the father
had a goodly sum, already, for service done to the
Heernocht lands, at the time of the great inundation.
Every week we had a guilder left over, sometimes
more; for the father worked extra hours, and could
get high pay for his labor. Every Saturday night
we put something by, except the time when you had
the fever, Hans, and when Gretel came. At last
the pouch grew so full that I mended an old stocking
and commenced again. Now that I look back, it
seems that the money was up to the heel in a few
sunny weeks. There was great pay in those days
if a man was quick at engineer work. The stocking
went on filling with copper and silver—aye, and
gold. You may well open your eyes, Gretel. I used
to laugh and tell the father it was not for poverty I
wore my old gown;—and the stocking went on filling
—so full that sometimes when I awoke at night, I'd
get up, soft and quiet, and go feel it in the moonlight.
Then, on my knees, I would thank our Lord that my
little ones could in time get good learning, and that
the father might rest from labor in his old age.
Sometimes, at supper, the father and I would talk
about a new chimney and a good winter-room for the
cow; but my man forsooth had finer plans even than

that. 'A big sail,' says he, 'catches the wind—we
can do what we will soon,' and then we would sing
together as I washed my dishes. Ah, 'a smooth sea
makes an easy rudder'—not a thing vexed me from
morning till night. Every week the father would
take out the stocking, and drop in the money and
laugh and kiss me as we tied it up together. Up
with you, Hans! there you sit gaping, and the day
a-wasting!" added Dame Brinker tartly, blushing to
find that she had been speaking too freely to her boy.
"It's high time you were on your way."

Hans had seated himself and was looking earnestly into her face. He arose, and, in almost a
whisper, asked:

"Have you ever tried, mother?"

"Yes, child, often. But the father only laughs, or
he stares at me so strange I am glad to ask no more.
When you and Gretel had the fever last Winter, and
our bread was nearly gone, and I could earn nothing,
for fear you would die while my face was turned,
oh! I tried then! I smoothed his hair, and whispered
to him soft as a kitten, about the money—where it
was—who had it? Alack! he would pick at my
sleeve, and whisper gibberish till my blood ran cold.
At last, while Gretel lay whiter than snow and you
were raving on the bed, I screamed to him—it seemed as if he must hear me—'Raff, where is our
money? Do you know aught of the money, Raff?—
the money in the pouch and the stocking, in the big
chest?'—but I might as well have talked to a stone
—I might as—"

The mother's voice sounded so strangely, and her
eye was so bright, that Hans, with a new anxiety,
laid his hand upon her shoulder.

"Come, mother," he said, "let us try to forget this

money. I am big and strong—Gretel, too, is very quick and willing. Soon all will be prosperous with us again. Why, mother, Gretel and I would rather see thee bright and happy, than to have all the silver in the world—wouldn't we, Gretel?"

"The mother knows it," said Gretel, sobbing.

CHAPTER VI

SUNBEAMS

Dame Brinker was startled at her children's emotion, glad, too, for it proved how loving and true they
were.

Beautiful ladies, in princely homes, often smile
suddenly and sweetly, gladdening the very air
around them; but I doubt if their smile be more welcome in God's sight than that which sprang forth to
cheer the roughly clad boy and girl in the humble
cottage. Dame Brinker felt that she had been selfish.
Blushing and brightening, she hastily wiped her
eyes, and looked upon them as only a mother can.

"Hoity! Toity! pretty talk we're having, and Saint
Nicholas' Eve almost here! What wonder the yarn
pricks my fingers! Come, Gretel, take this cent, and
while Hans is trading for the skates you can buy
a waffle in the market-place."

"Let me stay home with you, mother," said Gretel,
looking up with eyes that sparkled through their
tears. "Hans will buy me the cake."

"As you will, child, and Hans—wait a moment.
Three turns of the needle will finish this toe, and
then you may have as good a pair of hose as ever
were knitted, owning the yarn is a grain too sharp,
to sell to the hosier on the Heireen Gracht. That
will give us three quarter-guilders if you make good
trade; and as it's right hungry weather, you may
buy four waffles. We'll keep the Feast of Saint
Nicholas after all."

Gretel clapped her hands. "That will be fine!
Annie Bouman told me what grand times they will
have in the big house to-night. But we will be merry
too. Hans will have beautiful new skates—and then

there'll be the waffles! Oh-h! Don't break them,
brother Hans. Wrap them well, and button them
under your jacket very carefully."

"Certainly," replied Hans quite gruff with pleasure and importance.

"Come, Hans," she said, as her boy lingered by the
door, "what keeps thee?"

Hans kissed his mother's plump cheek, rosy and
fresh yet in spite of all her troubles—"my mother is
the best in the world, and I would be right glad to
have a pair of skates, but"—and, as he buttoned his
jacket, he looked, in a troubled way, toward a
strange figure crouching by the hearth-stone—"if
my money would bring a doctor from Amsterdam
to see the father, something might yet be done."

"A meester would not come, Hans, for twice that
money; and it would do no good if he did. Ah!
how many guilders I once spent for that; but the
dear, good father would not waken. It is God's will.
Go, Hans, and buy the skates."

Hans started with a heavy heart, but since the
heart was young, and in the boy's bosom, it set him
whistling in less than five minutes. His mother had
said "thee" to him, and that was quite enough to
make even a dark day sunny. Hollanders do not
address each other, in affectionate intercourse, as the
French and Germans do. But Dame Brinker had
embroidered for a heidelberg family in her girl-
hood, and she had carried its "thee" and "thou" into
her rude home, to be used in moments of extreme
love and tenderness.

Therefore, "What keeps thee, Hans?" sang an
echo song beneath the boy's whistling, and made him
feel that his errand was blessed.

Hans glanced toward the village, as he shook his
silver kwartes, and wondered whether it were really

true, as he had often heard, that some of the people of Broek were so rich that they used kitchen utensils of solid gold.

He had seen Mevrouw van Stoop's sweet-cheeses in market, and he knew that the lofty dame earned many a bright silver guilder in selling them. But did she set the cream to rise in golden pans? Did she use a golden skimmer? When her cows were in winter quarters, were their tails really tied up with ribbons?

These thoughts ran through his mind as he turned his face toward Amsterdam, not five miles away, on the other side of the frozen Y*. The ice upon the canal was perfect; but his wooden runners, so soon to be cast aside, squeaked a dismal farewell, as he scraped and skimmed along.

When crossing the Y, whom should he see skating toward him but the great Dr. Boekman, the most famous physician and surgeon in Holland. Hans had never met him before, but he had seen his engraved likeness in many of the shop-windows in Amsterdam. It was a face that one could never forget. Thin and lank, though a born Dutchman, with stern, blue eyes, and queer, compressed lips, that seemed to say "no smiling permitted," he certainly was not a very jolly or sociable looking personage, nor one that a well-trained boy would care to accost unbidden.

But Hans was bidden, and that, too, by a voice he seldom disregarded—his own conscience.

"Here comes the greatest doctor in the world," whispered the voice, "God has sent him; you have no right to buy skates when you might, with the same money, purchase such aid for your father!"

The wooden runners gave an exultant squeak.

*Pronounced Eye, an arm of the Zuider Zee.

Hundreds of beautiful skates were gleaming and vanishing in the air above him. He felt the money tingle in his fingers. The old doctor looked fearfully grim and forbidding. Hans' heart was in his throat, but he found voice enough to cry out, just as he was passing:

"Mynheer Boekman!"

The great man halted, and sticking out his thin under lip, looked scowling about him.

Hans was in for it now.

"Mynheer," he panted, drawing close to the fierce-looking doctor, "I knew you could be none other than the famous Boekman. I have to ask a great favor—"

"Humph!" muttered the doctor, preparing to skate past the intruder—"get out of my way—I've no money—never give to beggars."

"I am no beggar, Mynheer," retorted Hans proudly, at the same time producing his mite of silver with a grand air, "I wish to consult with you about my father. He is a living man, but sits like one dead. He cannot think. His words mean nothing— but he is not sick. He fell on the dikes."

"Hey? what?" cried the doctor beginning to listen.

Hans told the whole story in an incoherent way, dashing off a tear once or twice as he talked, and finally ending with an earnest—

"Oh, do see him, Mynheer. His body is well—it is only his mind—I know this money is not enough; but take it, Mynheer, I will earn more—I know I will—oh! I will toil for you all my life, if you will but cure my father!"

What was the matter with the old doctor? A brightness like sunlight beamed from his face. His eyes were kind and moist; the hand that had lately clutched his cane, as if preparing to strike, was laid gently upon Hans' shoulder.

"Put up your money, boy, I do not want it—we will see your father. It is a hopeless case, I fear. How long did you say?"

"Ten years, Mynheer," sobbed Hans, radiant with sudden hope.

"Ah! a bad case; but I shall see him. Let me think. To-day I start for Leyden, to return in a week, then you may expect me. Where is it?"

"A mile south of Broek, Mynheer, near the canal. It is only a poor broken-down hut. Any of the children thereabout can point it out to your honor," added Hans, with a heavy sigh; "they are all half afraid of the place; they call it the idiot's cottage."

"That will do," said the doctor, hurrying on, with a bright backward nod at Hans, "I shall be there. A hopeless case," he muttered to himself, "but the boy pleases me. His eye is like my poor Laurens. Confound it, shall I never forget that young scoundrel!" and, scowling more darkly than ever, the doctor pursued his silent way.

Again Hans was skating toward Amsterdam on the squeaking wooden runners; again his fingers tingled against the money in his pocket; again the boyish whistle rose unconsciously to his lips:

"Shall I hurry home," he was thinking, "to tell the good news, or shall I get the waffles and the new skates first? Whew! I think I'll go on!"

And so Hans bought the skates.

CHAPTER VII

INTRODUCING JACOB POOT AND HIS COUSIN

Hans and Gretel had a fine frolic early on that Saint Nicholas' Eve. There was a bright moon; and their mother, though she believed herself to be without any hope of her husband's improvement, had been made so happy at the prospect of the meester's visit, that she had yielded to the children's entreaties for an hour's skating before bedtime.

Hans was delighted with his new skates, and in his eagerness to show Gretel how perfectly they "worked" did many things upon the ice, that caused the little maid to clasp her hands in solemn admiration. They were not alone, though they seemed quite unheeded by the various groups assmbled upon the canal.

The two Van Holps and Carl Schummel were there, testing their fleetness to the utmost. Out of four trials Peter Van Holp had beaten three times. Consequently Carl, never very amiable, was in anything but a good humor. He had relieved himself by taunting young Schimmelpenninck who, being smaller than the others, kept meekly near them, without feeling exactly like one of the party; but now a new thought seized Carl, or rather he seized the new thought and made an onset upon his friends.

"I say, boys, let's put a stop to those young rag-pickers from the idiot's cottage joining the race. Hilda must be crazy to think of it. Katrinka Flack and Rychie Korbes are furious at the very idea of racing with the girl: and for my part, I don't blame them. As for the boy, if we've a spark of manhood in us we will scorn the very idea of—"

"Certainly we will!" interposed Peter Van Holp,

purposely mistaking Carl's meaning, "who doubts
it? No fellow with a spark of manhood in him would
refuse to let in two good skaters just because they
were poor!"

Carl wheeled about savagely—

"Not so fast, master! and I'd thank you not to
put words in other people's mouths. You'd best not
try it again."

"Ha! ha!" laughed little Voostenwalbert Schimmelpenninck, delighted at the prospect of a fight,
and sure that, if it should come to blows, his favorite
Peter could beat a dozen excitable fellows like Carl.

Something in Peter's eye made Carl glad to turn
to a weaker offender. He wheeled furiously upon
Voost.

"What are you shrieking about, you little weasel!
You skinny herring you, you little monkey with a
long name for a tail!"

Half a dozen by-standers and by-skaters set up an
applauding shout at this brave witticism; and Carl,
feeling that he had fairly vanquished his foes, was
restored to partial good humor. He, however, prudently resolved to defer plotting against Hans and
Gretel until some time when Peter should not be
present.

Just then, his friend, Jacob Poot, was seen approaching. They could not distinguish his features
at first; but as he was the stoutest boy in the neighborhood there could be no mistaking his form.

"Hola! here comes Fatty!" exclaimed Carl, "and,
there's some one with him, a slender fellow, a
stranger."

"Ha! ha! that's like good bacon," cried Ludwig;
"a streak of lean and a streak of fat."

"That's Jacob's English cousin," put in Master
Voost, delighted at being able to give the informa-

tion, "that's his English cousin, and, oh! he's got such a funny little name,—BEN DOBBS. He's going to stay with him until after the grand race."

All this time the boys had been spinning, turning, "rolling" and doing other feats upon their skates, in a quiet way, as they talked; but now they stood still, bracing themselves against the frosty air as Jacob Poot and his friend drew near.

"This is my cousin, boys," said Jacob, rather out of breath—"Benjamin Dobbs. He's a John Bull and he's going to be in the race."

All crowded, boy-fashion, about the newcomers. Benjamin soon made up his mind that the Hollanders, notwithstanding their queer gibberish, were a fine set of fellows.

Jacob and Ben had obtained permission to go on a long skating journey—no less a one than from Broek to the Hague, the capital of Holland, a distance of nearly fifty miles!*

"And now, boys," added Jacob, when he had told the plan, "who will go with us?"

"I will! I will!" cried the boys eagerly.

"And so will I," ventured little Voostenwalbert.

"Ha! ha!" laughed Jacob, holding his fat sides, and shaking his puffy cheeks, "*you* go? Such a little fellow as you? Why, youngster, you haven't left off your pads yet!"

Now in Holland very young children wear a thin, padded cushion around their heads, surmounted with a framework of whalebone and ribbon, to protect them in case of a fall; and it is the dividing line between babyhood and childhood when they leave it off. Voost had arrived at this dignity several years be-

*Throughout this narrative distances are given according to our standard, the English statute mile of 5,280 feet. The Dutch mile is more than four times as long as ours.

fore; consequently Jacob's insult was rather too great for endurance.

"Look out what you say!" he squeaked. "Lucky for you when you can leave off your pads—you're padded all over!"

"Ha! ha!" roared all the boys except Master Dobbs, who could not understand. "Ha! ha!"—and the good-natured Jacob laughed more than any.

"It ish my fat—yaw—he say I bees pad mit fat!" he explained to Ben.

So a vote was passed unanimously in favor of allowing the now popular Voost to join the party, if his parents would consent.

"Good-night!" sang out the happy youngster, skating homeward with all his might.

"Good-night!"

"We can stop at Haarlem, Jacob, and show your cousin the big organ," said Peter Van Holp, eagerly, "and at Leyden, too, where there's no end to the sights; and spend a day and night at the Hague, for my married sister, who lives there, will be delighted to see us; and the next morning we can start for home."

"All right!" responded Jacob, who was not much of a talker.

Ludwig had been regarding his brother with enthusiastic admiration.

"Hurrah for you, Pete! It takes you to make plans! Mother'll be as full of it as we are when we tell her we can take her love direct to sister Van Gend. My! but it's cold," he added, "cold enough to take a fellow's head off his shoulders. We'd better go home."

"What if it is cold, old Tender-skin?" cried Carl, who was busily practicing a step which he called the "double edge." "Great skating we should have by this time, if it was as warm as it was last December. Don't you know if it wasn't an extra cold winter, and an early one into the bargain, we couldn't go."

"I know it's an extra cold night anyhow," said Ludwig. "Whew! I'm going home!"

Peter Van Holp took out a bulgy gold watch, and holding it toward the moonlight as well as his benumbed fingers would permit, called out:

"Hello! it's nearly eight o'clock! Saint Nicholas is about by this time, and I, for one, want to see the little ones stare. Good-night!"

"Good-night!" cried one and all,—and off they started, shouting, singing, and laughing as they flew along.

Where were Gretel and Hans?

Ah! how suddenly joy sometimes comes to an end!

They had skated about an hour, keeping aloof from the others—quite contented with each other, and Gretel had exclaimed, "Ah, Hans, how beautiful! how fine! to think that we both have skates! I tell you the stork brought us good-luck!"—when they heard something!

It was a scream—a very faint scream! No one else upon the canal observed it, but Hans knew its meaning too well. Gretel saw him turn white in the moonlight as he busily tore off his skates.

"The father!" he cried, "he has frightened our mother!" and Gretel ran after him toward the house as rapidly as she could.

CHAPTER VIII

SIGHT-SEEING

"Are we all here?" cried Peter, in high glee, as the party assembled upon the canal early the next morning, equipped for their skating journey. "Let me see. As Jacob has made me captain, I must call the roll. Carl Schummel——. You here?"

"Ya!"

"Jacob Poot!"

"Ya!"

"Benjamin Dobbs!"

"Ya-a!"

"Lambert von Mounen!"

"Ya!"

["That's lucky! Couldn't get on without you, as you're the only one who can speak English.] Ludwig van Holp!"

"Ya!"

"Voostenwalbert Schimmelpenninck!"

No answer.

"Ah! the little rogue has been kept at home. Now, boys it's just eight o'clock—glorious weather, and the Y is as firm as a rock—we'll be at Amsterdam in thirty minutes. One, Two, Three, START!"

True enough, in less than half an hour they had crossed a dike of solid masonry, and were in the very heart of the great metropolis of the Netherlands—a walled city of ninety-five islands and nearly two hundred bridges. Although Ben had been there twice since his arrival in Holland, he saw much to excite wonder; but his Dutch comrades, having lived near by all their lives, considered it the most matter-of-course place in the world. Everything interested Ben; the tall houses with their forked chimneys and gable ends facing the street; the merchants' ware-

rooms, perched high up under the roofs of their
dwellings, with long, arm-like cranes hoisting and
lowering goods past the household windows; the
grand public buildings erected upon wooden piles
driven deep into the marshy ground; the narrow
streets; the canals everywhere crossing the city; the
bridges; the locks; the various costumes, and, strangest of all, shops and dwellings crouching close to the
fronts of the churches, sending their long, dispro-
portionate chimneys ·far upward along the sacred
walls.

If he looked up, he saw tall, leaning houses, seeming to pierce the sky with their shining roofs; if
he looked down, there was the queer street, without
crossing or curb—nothing to separate the cobble-
stone pavement from the foot-path of brick—and if
he rested his eyes half way, he saw complicated little
mirrors [*spionnen*] fastened upon the outside of
nearly every window, so arranged that the inmates
of the houses could observe all that was going on
in the street, or inspect whoever might be knocking
at the door, without being seen themselves.

Sometimes a dog-cart, heaped with wooden ware,
passed him; then a donkey bearing a pair of pan-
niers filled with crockery or glass; then a sled driven
over the bare cobble-stones (the runners kept
greased with a dripping oil rag so that it might run
easily) ; and then, perhaps, a showy, but clumsy fam-
ily-carriage, drawn by the brownest of Flanders
horses, swinging the whitest of snowy tails.

"Shall we go on by the canal or the river?" asked
Peter.

"Oh, the river, by all means," said Carl. "It will
be such fun; they say it is perfect skating all the
way, but it's much farther."

Jacob Poot instantly became interested.

"I vote for the canal!" he cried.

"Well, the canal it shall be," responded the captain, "if all are agreed."

"Agreed!" they echoed, in rather a disappointed tone—and Captain Peter led the way.

"All right—come on—we can reach Haarlem in an hour!"

While skating along at full speed, they heard the cars from Amsterdam coming close behind them.

"Hollo!" cried Ludwig, glancing toward the rail-track—"who can't beat a locomotive? Let's give it a race!"

The whistle screamed at the very idea—so did the boys—and at it they went.

For an instant the boys were ahead, hurrahing with all their might—only for an instant, but even that was something.

This excitement over, they began to travel more leisurely, and indulge in conversation and frolic. Sometimes they stopped to exchange a word with the guards who were stationed at certain distances along the canal. These men, in Winter, attend to keeping the surface free from obstruction, and garbage. After a snow-storm they are expected to sweep the feathery covering away before it hardens into a marble pretty to look at but very unwelcome to skaters. Now and then the boys so far forgot their dignity as to clamber among the ice-bound canal-boats crowded together in a widened harbor off the canal, but the watchful guards would soon spy out them and order them down with a growl.

Nothing could be straighter than the canal upon which our party was skating, and nothing straighter than the long rows of willow trees that stood, bare and wispy, along the bank. On the opposite side, lifted high above the surrounding country lay the carriage road on top of the great dike built to keep Haarlem Lake within bounds; stretching out far in the distance until it became lost in a point, was the glassy canal with its many skaters, its brown-winged ice-boats, its push-chairs and its queer little sleds, light as cork, flying over the ice by means of iron-pronged sticks in the hands of the riders. Ben was in ecstasy with the scene.

Notwithstanding the absorbing interest of scenes along the way, there was much to talk about in their history, so time went with the speed of their skates. "It is strange to have such a warm feeling for such a cold place," exclaimed Ben. "If we were not exercising all the time we should freeze outright."

Lambert laughed.

"That's your English blood, Benjamin, I'm not cold. And look at the skaters here on the canal— they're red as roses, and happy as lords. Hallo! good Captain van Holp," called out Lambert in Dutch, "what say you to stopping at yonder farm-house and warming our toes?"

"Who is cold?" asked Peter, turning around.

"Benjamin Dobbs."

"Benjamin Dobbs shall be warmed," and the party was brought to a halt.

CHAPTER IX

ON THE WAY TO HAARLEM

On approaching the door of the farm-house the boys suddenly found themselves in the midst of a lively domestic scene. A burly Dutchman came rushing out, closely followed by his dear vrouw, and she was beating him smartly with a long handled warming pan. The expression on her face gave our boys so little promise of a kind reception that they prudently resolved to carry their toes elsewhere to be warmed.

The next cottage proved to be more inviting. Its low roof of bright red tiles, extended over the cow-stable, that, clean as could be, nestled close to the main building. A neat, peaceful-looking old woman sat at one window, knitting. At the other could be discerned part of the profile of a fat figure that, pipe in mouth, sat behind the shining little panes and snowy curtain. In answer to Peter's subdued knock, a fair-haired, rosy-cheeked lass in holiday attire opened the upper half of the green door (which was divided across the middle) and inquired their errand.

"May we enter and warm ourselves, jufvrouw?" asked the captain respectfully.

"Yes, and welcome," was the reply, as the lower half of the door swung softly toward its mate. Every boy before entering rubbed long and faithfully upon the rough mat, and each made his best bow to the old lady and gentleman at the windows. Ben was half inclined to think that these personages were automata like the moving figures in the garden at Broek; for they both nodded their heads slowly, in precisely the same way, and both went on with their employment as steadily and stiffly as though they worked by machinery. The old man puffed! puffed! and his vrouw clicked her knitting-needles, as if regulated by internal cog-wheels. Even the real smoke issuing from the motionless pipe gave no convincing proof that they were human.

But the rosy-cheeked maiden. Ah! how she bustled about. How she gave the boys polished high-backed chairs to sit upon, how she made the fire blaze as if it were inspired, how she made Jacob Poot almost weep for joy by bringing forth a great square of gingerbread, and a stone jug of sour wine! How she laughed and nodded as the boys ate like wild animals on good behavior, and how blank she looked when Ben politely but firmly refused to take any black bread and sourkrout! How she pulled off Jacob's mitten, which was torn at the thumb, and mended it before his eyes, biting off the thread with her teeth, and saying, "now it will be warmer," as she bit; and finally, how she shook hands with every boy in turn and (throwing a deprecating glance at the female automaton) insisted upon filling their pockets with gingerbread!

All this time the knitting needles clicked on, and the pipe never missed a puff.

When the boys were fairly on their way again, they came in sight of Zwanenburg Castle with its massive stone front, and its gate-way towers, each surmounted with a sculptured swan.

"Halfweg,* boys," said Peter, "off with your skates."

"You see," explained Lambert to his companion, "the Y and the Haarlem Lake meeting here make it rather troublesome. The river is five feet higher than the land—so we must have everything strong

*Half way.

in the way of dikes and sluice-gates, or there would be wet work at once. The sluice arrangements here are supposed to be something extra—we will walk over them and you shall see enough to make you open your eyes. The spring water of the lake, they say, has the most wonderful bleaching powers of any in the world; all the great Haarlem bleacheries use it. I can't say much upon that subject—but I can tell you one thing from personal experience."

"What is that?"

"Why the lake is full of the biggest eels you ever saw—I've caught them here, often—perfectly prodigious! I tell you they're sometimes a match for a fellow, they'd almost wriggle your arm from the socket if you were not on your guard. But you're not interested in eels, I perceive. The castle's a big affair. Isn't it?"

"Yes. What do those swans mean? Anything?" asked Ben, looking up at the stone gate-towers.

"The swan is held almost in reverence by us Hollanders. These give the building its name, Zwanenburg—swan-castle. That is all I know. This is a very important spot; for it is here that the wise ones hold council with regard to dike matters. The castle was once the residence of the celebrated Christiaan Brunings."

"What about him?" asked Ben.

"Peter could answer you better than I," said Lambert, "if you could only understand each other, or were not such cowards about leaving your mother-tongues. But I have often heard my grandfather speak of Brunings. He is never tired of telling us of the great engineer—how good he was, and how learned, and how when he died the whole country seemed to mourn as for a friend. He belonged to a great many learned societies, and was at the head

of the State department intrusted with the care of
the dikes, and other defenses against the sea.
There's no counting the improvements he made in
dikes and sluices and water-mills, and all that kind
of thing. We Hollanders, you know, consider our
great engineers as the highest of public benefactors.
Brunings died years ago; they've a monument to
his memory in the cathedral of Haarlem. I have
seen his portrait, and I tell you, Ben, he was right
noble-looking. No wonder the castle looks so stiff
and proud. It is something to have given shelter
to such a man!"

"Yes, indeed!" said Ben. "I wonder, Van Mounen, whether you or I will ever give any old building a right to feel proud—Heigho! there's a great
deal to be done yet in this world and some of us
who are boys now, will have to do it. Look to your
shoe latchet, Van, it's unfastened."

CHAPTER X

A CATASTROPHE

It was nearly one o'clock when Captain Van Holp and his command entered the grand old city of Haarlem. They had skated nearly seventeen miles since morning, and were still as fresh as young eagles. From the youngest (Ludwig van Holp, who was just fourteen) to the eldest, no less a personage . than the captain himself, a veteran of seventeen, there was but one opinion—that this was the greatest frolic of their lives. To be sure, Jacob Poot had become rather short of breath, during the last mile or two, and perhaps he felt ready for another nap; but there was enough jollity in him yet for a dozen. Even Carl Schummel, who had become very intimate with Ludwig during the excursion, forgot to be illnatured. As for Peter, he was the happiest of the happy, and had sung and whistled so joyously while skating that the staidest passers-by had smiled as they listened.

"Come boys! it's nearly tiffin*-hour," he said, as they neared a coffee-house on the main street. "We must have something more solid than the pretty maiden's gingerbread—" and the captain plunged his hands into his pockets as if to say "there's money enough here to feed an army!"

"Hello!" cried Lambert, "what ails the man?"

Peter, pale and staring, was clapping his hands upon his breast and sides—he looked like one suddenly becoming deranged.

"He's sick!" cried Ben.

"No, he's lost something," said Carl.

*Lunch.

Peter could only gasp—"the pocket book! with all our money in it—it's gone!"

For an instant all were too much startled to speak.

Carl at last came out with a gruff "No sense in letting one fellow have all the money. I said so from the first. Look in your other pocket."

"I did—it isn't there."

"Open your under jacket—"

Peter obeyed mechanically. He even took off his hat and looked into it—then thrust his hand desperately into every pocket.

"It's gone, boys," he said at last, in a hopeless tone. "No tiffin for us, nor dinner either. What is to be done? We can't get on without money. If we were in Amsterdam I could get as much as we want, but there is not a man in Haarlem from whom I can borrow a stiver. Don't any of you know any one here who would lend us a few guilders?"

Each boy looked into five blank faces. Then something like a smile passed around the circle, but it got sadly knotted up when it reached Carl.

"That wouldn't do," he said crossly, "I know some people here, rich ones, too, but father would flog me soundly, if I borrowed a cent from any one. He has 'AN HONEST MAN NEED NEVER BORROW' written over the gateway of his summer-house."

"Humph!" responded Peter, not particularly admiring the sentiment just at that moment.

The boys grew desperately hungry at once.

"It wash my fault," said Jacob, in a penitent tone, to Ben. "I say first, petter all de boys put zair pursh into Van Holp's monish."

"Nonsense, Jacob; you did it all for the best."

Ben said this in such a sprightly tone that the two Van Holps and Carl felt sure he had proposed a plan that would relieve the party at once.

"What? what? Tell us, Van Mounen," they cried.

"He says it is not Jacob's fault that the money is lost—that he did it for the best, when he proposed that Van Holp should put all of our money into his purse."

"Is that all?" said Ludwig dismally, "he need not have made such a fuss in just saying that. How much money have we lost?"

"Don't you remember?" said Peter. "We each put in exactly ten guilders. The purse had sixty guilders in it. I am the stupidest fellow in the world; little Schimmelpenninck would have made you a better captain. I could pommel myself for bringing such a disappointment upon you."

"Do it then," growled Carl. "Pooh," he added, "we all know it was an accident, but that doesn't help matters. We must have money, Van Holp— even if you have to sell your wonderful watch."

"Sell my mother's birthday present! Never! I will sell my coat, my hat, anything but my watch."

"Come, come," said Jacob pleasantly, "we are making too much of this affair. We can go home and start again in a day or two."

"You may be able to get another ten-guilder piece," said Carl, "but the rest of us will not find it so easy. If we go home, we stay home, you may depend."

Our captain, whose good-nature had not yet forsaken him for a moment, grew indignant.

"Do you think I will let you suffer for my carelessness," he exclaimed, "I have three times sixty guilders in my strong box at home!"

"Oh, I beg your pardon," said Carl, hastily, adding in a surlier tone, "well, I see no better way than to go back hungry."

"I see a better plan than that," said the Captain.
"What is it?" cried all the boys.

"Why, to make the best of a bad business and go back pleasantly, and like men," said Peter, looking so gallant and handsome as he turned his frank face and clear blue eyes upon them—that they caught his spirit.

"Ho! for the Captain," they shouted.

"Now, boys, we may as well make up our minds there's no place like Broek, after all—and that we mean to be there in two hours—is that agreed to?"

"Agreed!" cried all, as they ran to the canal.

"On with your skates! Are you ready? Here, Jacob, let me help you."

"Now. One, two, three, start!"

And the boyish faces that left Haarlem at that signal were nearly as bright as those that had entered it with Captain Peter half an hour before.

CHAPTER XI

HANS

"Donder and Blixin!" cried Carl angrily, before the party had skated twenty yards from the city gates, "if here isn't that wooden-skate ragamuffin in the patched leather breeches. That fellow is everywhere, confound him. We'll be lucky," he added, in as sneering a tone as he dared assume, "if our captain doesn't order us to halt and shake hands with him."

"Your captain is a terrible fellow," said Peter, pleasantly "but this is a false alarm, Carl—I cannot spy your bugbear anywhere among the skaters—ah! there he is! why what is the matter with the lad?"

Poor Hans! His face was pale, his lips compressed. He skated like one under the effects of a fearful dream. Just as he was passing, Peter hailed him:

"Good-day, Hans Brinker!"

Hans' countenance brightened at once—"Ah, mynheer, is that you? It is well we meet!"

"Just like his impertinence," hissed Carl Schummel, darting scornfully past his companions, who seemed inclined to linger with their captain.

"I am glad to see you, Hans," responded Peter, cheerily, "but you look troubled. Can I serve you?"

"I have a trouble, mynheer," answered Hans, casting down his eyes. Then lifting them again with almost a happy expression, he added, "but it is Hans who can help Mynheer van Holp this time."

"How?" asked Peter, making, in his blunt Dutch way, no attempt to conceal his surprise.

"By giving you this, mynheer"—and Hans held forth the missing purse.

"Hurrah!" shouted the boys, taking their cold hands from their pockets to wave them joyfully in the air. But Peter said "thank you, Hans Brinker," in a tone that made Hans feel as if the king had knelt to him.

The shout of the delighted boys reached the muffled ears of the fine young gentleman who, under a full pressure of pent-up wrath, was skating toward Amsterdam. A Yankee boy would have wheeled about at once and hastened to satisfy his curiosity. But Carl only halted, and with his back toward his party wondered what on earth had happened. There he stood, immovable, until, feeling sure that nothing but the prospect of something to eat could have made them hurrah so heartily, he turned and skated slowly toward his excited comrades.

Meantime Peter had drawn Hans aside from the rest.

"How did you know it was my purse?" he asked.

"You paid me three guilders yesterday, mynheer, for making the white-wood chain, telling me that I must buy skates."

"Yes, I remember."

"I saw your purse then; it was of yellow leather."

"And where did you find it to-day?"

"I left my home this morning, mynheer, in great trouble, and as I skated, I took no heed until I stumbled against some lumber, and while I was rubbing my knee I saw your purse nearly hidden under a log."

"That place! Ah, I remember, now; just as we were passing it I pulled my tippet from my pocket, and probably flirted out the purse at the same time. It would have been gone but for you, Hans. Here" —pouring out the contents—"you must give us the pleasure of dividing the money with you—"

"No, mynheer," answered Hans. He spoke quietly, without pretense, or any grace of manner, but Peter, somehow, felt rebuked, and put the silver back without a word.

"I like that boy, rich or poor," he thought to himself, then added aloud, "May I ask about this trouble of yours, Hans?"

"Ah, mynheer, it is a sad case—but I have waited here too long. I am going to Leyden to see the great Doctor Boekman—"

"Doctor Boekman!" exclaimed Peter in astonishment.

"Yes, mynheer, and I have not a moment to lose. Good-day!"

"Stay, I am going that way. Come, my lads! Shall we return to Haarlem?"

"Yes," cried the boys, eagerly—and off they started.

"Now," said Peter, drawing near Hans, both skimming the ice so easily and lightly as they skated on together that they seemed scarce conscious of moving, "we are going to stop at Leyden, and if you are going there only with a message to Doctor Boekman cannot I do the earrand for you? The boys may be too tired to skate so far to-day, but I will promise to see him early to-morrow if he is to be found in the city."

"Ah, mynheer, that would be serving me indeed; it is not the distance I dread, but leaving my mother so long."

"Is she ill?"

"No, mynheer. It is the father. You may have heard it; how he has been without wit for many a year—ever since the great Schlossen mill was built; but his body has been well and strong. Last night, the mother knelt upon the hearth to blow the peat (it is his only delight to sit and watch the live embers; and she will blow them into a blaze every hour of the day to please him). Before she could stir, he sprang upon her like a giant and held her close to the fire, all the time laughing and shaking his head. I was on the canal; but I heard the mother scream and ran to her. The father had never loosened his hold, and her gown was smoking. I tried to deaden the fire, but with one hand he pushed me off. There was no water in the cottage or I could have done better—and all that time he laughed—such a terrible laugh, mynheer; hardly a sound, but all in his face—I tried to pull her away, but that only made it worse—then—it was dreadful, but could I see the mother burn? I beat him—beat him with a stool. He tossed me away. The gown was on fire! I would put it out. I can't remember well after that; I found myself upon the floor and the mother was praying—It seemed to me that she was in a blaze, and all the while I could hear that laugh. My sister Gretel screamed out that he was holding the mother close to the very coals. I could not tell! Gretel flew to the closet and filled a porringer with the food he liked, and put it upon the floor. Then, mynheer, he left the mother and crawled to it like a little child. She was not burnt, only a part of her clothing—ah, how kind she was to him all night, watching and tending him—He slept in a high fever, with his hands pressed to his head. The mother says he has done that so much of late, as though he felt pain there—ah, mynheer, I did not mean to tell you. If the father was himself, he would not harm even a kitten—"

For a moment the two boys moved on in silence—

"It is terrible," said Peter at last—"How is he to-day?"

"Very sick, mynheer!"

"Why go for Dr. Boekman, Hans? There are others in Amsterdam who could help him, perhaps: —Boekman is a famous man, sought only by the wealthiest and they often wait upon him in vain."

"He promised, mynheer, he promised me yesterday to come to the father in a week—but now that the change has come, we cannot wait—we think the poor father is dying!—Oh, mynheer, you can plead with him to come quick—he will not wait a whole week and our father dying—the good meester is so kind—"

"So kind!" echoed Peter, in astonishment, "why he is known as the crossest man in Holland!"

"He looks so because he has no fat, and his head is busy but his heart is kind, I know—Tell the meester what I have told you, mynheer, and he will come."

"I hope so, Hans, with all my heart. You are in haste to turn homeward I see. Promise me that should you need a friend, you will go to my mother, at Broek. Tell her I bade you see her; and, Hans Brinker—not as a reward—but as a gift—take a few of these guilders."

Hans shook his head resolutely.

"No, no, mynheer—I cannot take it. If I could find work in Broek or at the South Mill I would be glad, but it is the same story everywhere—'wait till Spring'."

"It is well you speak of it," said Peter eagerly, "for my father needs help at once—Your pretty chain pleased him much—he said 'that boy has a clean cut, he would be good at carving'—There is to be a carved portal to our new summer-house, and father will pay well for the job."

"God is good!" cried Hans in sudden delight—
"Oh! mynheer, that would be too much joy—I have
never tried big work—but I can do it—I know I
can."

"Well, tell my father you are the Hans Brinker of
whom I spoke. He will be glad to serve you."

Hans stared in honest surprise.

"Thank you, mynheer."

"Now, Captain," shouted Carl, anxious to appear
as good-humored as possible, by way of atonement,
"here we are in the midst of Haarlem, and no word
from you yet—we await your orders, and we're as
hungry as wolves."

Peter made a cheerful answer, and turned hurriedly to Hans.

"Come get something to eat, and I will detain
you no longer."

What a quick, wistful look Hans threw upon him!
Peter wondered that he had not noticed before that
the poor boy was hungry.

"Ah, mynheer, even now the mother may need
me, the father may be worse—I must not wait—May
God care for you"—and, nodding hastily, Hans
turned his face homeward and was gone.

"Come, boys," sighed Peter, "now for our tiffin!"

CHAPTER XII

HOMES

It must not be supposed that our young Dutchmen
had already forgotten the great skating-race which
was to take place on the Twentieth. On the contrary,
they had thought and spoken of it very often during
the day. Even Ben, though he had felt more like a
traveler than the rest, had never once, through all
the sight-seeing, lost a certain vision of silver skates
which, for a week past, had haunted him night and
day.

Like a true "John Bull," as Jacob had called him,
he never doubted that his English fleetness, English
strength, English everything, could at any time enable him, on the ice, to put all Holland to shame, and
the rest of the world, too, for that matter. Ben
certainly was a superb skater. He had enjoyed
not half the opportunities for practising that had
fallen to his new comrades; but he had improved his
share to the utmost; and was, besides, so strong of
frame, so supple of limb—in short such a tight,
trim, quick, graceful fellow in every way, that he
had taken to skating as naturally as a chamois to
leaping, or an eagle to soaring.

Only to the heavy heart of poor Hans had the
vision of the silver skates failed to appear during
that starry Winter night and the brighter sunlit day.

Even Gretel had seen them flitting before her as
she sat beside her mother through those hours of
weary watching—not as prizes to be won, but as
treasures passing hopelessly beyond her reach.

Rychie, Hilda and Katrinka—why they had
scarcely known any other thought than "the race!
the race! It will come off on the Twentieth!"

These three girls were friends. Though of nearly the same age, talent and station, they were as different as girls could be.

Hilda Van Gleck you already know, a warm-hearted, noble girl of fourteen. Rychie Korbes was beautiful to look upon, far more sparkling and pretty than Hilda, but not half so bright and sunny within. Clouds of pride, of discontent and envy had already gathered in her heart, and were growing bigger and darker every day. Of course these often relieved themselves very much after the manner of other clouds—But who saw the storms and the weeping? Only her maid, or her father, mother and little brother—those who loved her better than all. Like other clouds, too, hers often took queer shapes, and what was really but mist and vapory fancy, assumed the appearance of monster wrongs and mountains of difficulty. To her mind, the poor peasant girl Gretel was not a human being, a God-created creature like herself—she was only something that meant poverty, rags and dirt. Such as Gretel had no right to feel, to hope; above all, they should never cross the paths of their betters—that is, not in a disagreeable way. They could toil and labor for them at a respectful distance, even admire them, if they would do it humbly, but nothing more. If they rebel, put them down —if they suffer, don't trouble me about it, was Rychie's secret motto. And yet how witty she was, how tastefully she dressed, how charmingly she sang; how much feeling she displayed (for pet kittens and rabbits), and how completely she could bewitch sensible, honest-minded lads like Lambert van Mounen and Ludwig van Holp!

Carl was too much like her, within, to be an earnest admirer, and perhaps he suspected the clouds. He, being deep and surly, and always uncomfortably in earnest, of course preferred the lively Katrinka, whose nature was made of a hundred tinkling bells. She was a coquette in her infancy, a coquette in her childhood, and now a coquette in her school days. Without a thought of harm she coquetted with her studies, her duties, even her little troubles. They shouldn't know when they bothered her, not they. She coquetted with her mother, her pet lamb, her baby brother, even with her own golden curls—tossing them back as if she despised them. Everyone liked her, but who could love her? She was never in earnest. A pleasant face, a pleasant heart, a pleasant manner—these only satisfy for an hour. Poor, happy Katrinka! such as she tinkle, tinkle so merrily through their early days; but Life is so apt to coquette with them in turn, to put all their sweet bells out of tune, or to silence them one by one!

How different were the homes of these three girls from the tumbling old cottage where Gretel dwelt. Rychie lived in a beautiful house near Amsterdam, where the carved side-boards were laden with services of silver and gold, and where silken tapestries hung in folds from ceiling to floor.

Hilda's father owned the largest mansion in Broek. Its glittering roof of polished tiles, and its boarded front, painted in half a dozen various colors, were the admiration of the neighborhood.

Katrinka's home, not a mile distant, was the finest of Dutch country-seats. The garden was so stiffly laid out in little paths and patches that the birds might have mistaken it for a great Chinese puzzle with all the pieces spread out ready for use. But in Summer it was beautiful; flowers made the best of their stiff quarters, and, when the gardener was not watching, glowed and bent and twined about each other in the prettiest way imaginable. Such a tulip bed! Why, the Queen of the Fairies would never care for a grander city in which to hold her court! but Katrinka preferred the bed of pink and white hyacinths. She loved their freshness and fragrance, and the light-hearted way in which their bell-shaped blossoms swung in the breeze.

Carl was both right and wrong when he said that Katrinka and Rychie were furious at the very idea of the peasant Gretel joining in the race. He had heard Rychie declare it was "disgraceful, shameful, TOO BAD!" which in Dutch, as in English, is generally the strongest expression an indignant girl can use; and he had seen Katrinka nod her pretty head, and heard her sweetly echo "shameful, too bad!" as nearly like Rychie as tinkling bells can be like the voice of real anger. This had satisfied him. He never suspected that had Hilda, not Rychie, first talked with Katrinka upon the subject, the bells would have jingled as willing an echo. She would have said "certainly, let her join us," and would have skipped off thinking no more about it. But now Katrinka with sweet emphasis pronounced it a shame that a goose-girl, a forlorn little creature like Gretel, should be allowed to spoil the race.

Rychie being rich and powerful (in a school-girl way) had other followers, besides Katrinka, who were induced to share her opinions because they were either too careless or too cowardly to think for themselves.

Poor little Gretel! Her home was sad and dark enough now. Raff Brinker lay moaning upon his rough bed, and his vrouw, forgetting and forgiving everything, bathed his forehead, his lips, weeping and praying that he might not die. Hans, as we know, had started, in desperation, for Leyden to search for Dr. Boekman, and induce him, if possible, to come to their father at once. Gretel, filled with a strange dread, had done the work as well as she could, wiped the rough brick floor, brought peat to build up the slow fire, and melted ice for her mother's use. This accomplished, she seated herself upon a low stool near the bed, and begged her mother to try and sleep awhile.

"You are so tired," she whispered, "not once have you closed your eyes since that dreadful hour last night. See, I have straightened the willow bed in the corner, and spread everything soft upon it I could find, so that the mother might lie in comfort. Here is your jacket. Take off that pretty dress, I'll fold it away very careful, and put it in the big chest before you go to sleep."

Dame Brinker shook her head without turning her eyes from her husband's face.

"I can watch, mother," urged Gretel, "and I'll wake you every time the father stirs. You are so pale, and your eyes are so red—oh, mother, *do!*"

The child pleaded in vain. Dame Brinker would not leave her post.

Gretel looked at her in troubled silence, wondering whether it were very wicked to care more for one parent than for the other—and sure, yes, quite sure, that she dreaded her father, while she clung to her mother with a love that was almost idolatry.

"Hans loves the father so well," she thought, "why cannot I? Yet I could not help crying when I saw his hand bleed that day, last month, when he snatched the knife—and now, when he moans, how I ache, ache all over. Perhaps I love him, after all, and God will see I am not such a bad, wicked girl as I thought. Yes, I love the poor father—almost as Hans does—not quite, for Hans is stronger and does not fear him. Oh, will that moaning go on forever and ever! Poor mother, how patient she is; she never pouts, as I do, about the money that went away so strange. If he only could, just for one instant, open his eyes and look at us, as Hans does, and tell us where mother's guilders went, I would not care for the rest—yes, I would care—I don't want the poor father to die, to be all blue and cold like Annie Bouman's little sister—I know I don't —dear God, I don't want father to die."

Her thoughts merged into a prayer. When it ended, the poor child scarcely knew. Soon she found herself watching a little pulse of light at the side of the fire, beating faintly but steadily, showing that somewhere in the dark pile there was warmth and light that would overspread it at last. A large earthen cup filled with burning peat stood near the bed-side; Gretel had placed it there to "stop the father's shivering," she said. She watched it as it sent a glow around the mother's form, tipping her faded skirt with light, and shedding a sort of newness over the threadbare bodice. It was a relief to Gretel to see the lines in that weary face soften as the fire-light flickered gently across it.

Next she counted the window-panes, broken and patched as they were; and finally, after tracing every crack and seam in the walls, fixed her gaze upon a carved shelf made by Hans. The shelf hung as high as Gretel could reach. It held a large leather-covered Bible, with brass clasps, a wedding present to Dame Brinker from the family at Heidelberg.

"Ah, how handy Hans is! If he were here he could turn the father some way so the moans would stop—dear! dear! if this sickness lasts, we shall never skate any more. I must send my new skates back to the beautiful lady. Hans and I will not see the race," and Gretel's eyes, that had been dry before, grew full of tears.

"Never cry, child," said the mother soothingly. "This sickness may not be as bad as we think. The father has lain this way before."

Gretel sobbed now.

"Oh, mother, it is not that alone—you do not know all—I am very, very bad and wicked!"

"You, Gretel! you so patient and good!" and a bright, puzzled look beamed for an instant upon the child. "Hush, lovely, you'll wake him."

Gretel hid her face in her mother's lap and tried not to cry.

Her little hand, so thin and brown, lay in the coarse palm of her mother, creased with many a hard day's work. Rychie would have shuddered to touch either, yet they pressed warmly upon each other. Soon Gretel looked up with that dull, homely look which, they say, poor children in shanties are apt to have, and said in a trembling voice:

"The father tried to burn you—he did—I saw him, and he was laughing!"

"Hush, child!"

The mother's words came so suddenly and sharply, that Raff Brinker, dead as he was to all that was passing round him, twitched slightly upon the bed.

Gretel said no more, but plucked drearily at the jagged edge of a hole in her mother's holiday gown. It had been burned there—well for Dame Brinker that the gown was woolen.

CHAPTER XIII

HAARLEM—THE BOYS HEAR VOICES

Refreshed and rested, our boys came forth from the coffee-house just as the big clock in the Square, after the manner of certain Holland time-keepers, was striking TWO with its half-hour bell, for half-past TWO.

The captain was absorbed in thought, at first, for Hans Brinker's sad story still echoed in his ears. Not until Ludwig rebuked him with a laughing "Wake up, Grandfather!" did he re-assume his position as gallant boy-leader of his band.

"Ahem! this way, young gentlemen!"

They were walking through the streets of the city, not on a curbed sidewalk, for such a thing is rarely to be found in Holland, but on the brick pavement that lay on the borders of the cobble-stone carriage-way without breaking its level expanse.

Haarlem, like Amsterdam, was gayer than usual, in honor of St. Nicholas.

A strange figure was approaching them. It was a small man dressed in black, with a short cloak; he wore a wig and a cocked hat from which a long crepe streamer was flying.

"Who comes here?" cried Ben, "what a queer-looking object."

"That's the aanspreeker," said Lambert, "some one is dead."

"Is that the way men dress in mourning in this country?"

"Oh, no. The aanspreeker attends funerals, and it is his business, when any one dies, to notify all the friends and relatives."

"What a strange custom."

"Well," said Lambert, "we needn't feel very badly about this particular death, for I see another man has lately been born to the world to fill up the vacant place."

Ben stared. "How do you know that?"

"Don't you see that pretty red pin-cushion hanging on yonder door?" asked Lambert in return.

"Yes."

"Well, that's a boy."

"A boy! What do you mean?"

"I mean that here in Haarlem whenever a boy is born the parents have a red pin-cushion put out at the door. If our young friend had been a girl instead of a boy the cushion would have been white. In some places they have much more fanciful affairs, all trimmed with lace, and even among the very poorest houses you will see a bit of ribbon or even a string tied on the door latch—"

"Look!" almost screamed Ben, "there is a white cushion at the door of that double-jointed house with the funny roof."

"I don't see any house with a funny roof."

"Oh, of course not," said Ben, "I forget you're a native; but all the roofs are queer to me, for that matter. I mean the house next to that green building."

"True enough—there's a girl! I tell you what, captain, called out Lambert, slipping easily into Dutch, "we must get out of this street as soon as possible. It's full of babies! They'll set up a squall in a moment."

The captain laughed. "I shall take you to hear better music than that," he said; "we are just in time to hear the organ of St. Bavon. The church is open today."

"What, the great Haarlem organ?" asked Ben.

"That will be a treat indeed. I have often read of it, with its tremendous pipes, and its *vox humana* that sounds like a giant singing."

"The same," answered Lambert van Mounen.

Peter was right. The church was open, though not for religious services. Some one was playing upon the organ. As the boys entered, a swell of sound rushed forth to meet them. It seemed to bear them, one by one, into the shadows of the building.

Louder and louder it grew until it became like the din and roar of some mighty tempest, or like the ocean surging upon the shore. In the midst of the tumult a tinkling bell was heard; another answered, then another, and the storm paused as if to listen. The bells grew bolder; they rang out loud and clear. Other deep toned bells joined in; they were tolling in solemn concert—ding, dong! ding, dong! The storm broke forth again with redoubled fury—gathering its distant thunder. The boys looked at each other, but did not speak. It was growing serious. What was that? Who screamed? What screamed—that terrible, musical scream? Was it man or demon? Or was it some monster shut up behind that carved brass frame—behind those great silver columns—some despairing monster begging, screaming for freedom? It was the Vox Humana!

At last an answer came, soft, tender, loving, like a mother's song. The storm grew silent; hidden birds sprang forth filling the air with glad, ecstatic music, rising higher and higher until the last faint note was lost in the distance.

The Vox Humana was stilled; but in the glorious hymn of thanksgiving that now arose, one could almost hear the throbbing of a human heart. What did it mean? That man's imploring cry should in

time be met with a deep content? That gratitude
would give us freedom? To Peter and Ben it seemed that the angels were singing. Their eyes grew
dim, and their souls dizzy with a strange joy. At
last, as if borne upward by invisible hands, they
were floating away on the music, all fatigue forgotten, and with no wish but to hear forever those beautiful sounds—when suddenly Van Holp's sleeve was
pulled impatiently and a gruff voice beside him
asked:

"How long are you going to stay here, captain—
blinking at the ceiling like a sick rabbit? It's high
time we started."

"Hush!" whispered Peter, only half aroused.

"Come, man! Let's go," said Carl, giving the
sleeve a second pull.

Peter turned reluctantly; he would not detain the
boys against their will. All but Ben were casting
rather reproachful glances upon him.

"Well, boys," he whispered, "we will go. Softly
now."

"That's the greatest thing I've seen or heard since
I've been in Holland!" cried Ben, enthusiastically,
as soon as they reached the open air. "It's glorious!"

Ludwig and Carl laughed slyly at the English
boy's *wartaal*, or gibberish; Jacob yawned; Peter
gave Ben a look that made him instantly feel that he
and Peter were not so very different after all, though
one hailed from Holland and the other from England; and Lambert, the interpreter, responded with
a brisk—

"You may well say so. I believe there are one or
two organs now-a-days that are said to be as fine;
but for years and years this organ of St. Bavon was
the grandest in the world."

"Do you know how large it is?" asked Ben. "I noticed that the church itself was prodigiously high and that the organ filled the end of the great aisle almost from floor to roof."

"That's true," said Lambert, "and how superb the pipes looked—just like grand columns of silver. They're only for show, you know; the real pipes are behind them, some big enough for a man to crawl through, and some smaller than a baby's whistle. Well, sir, for size, the church is higher than Westminster Abbey, to begin with, and, as you say, the organ makes a tremendous show even then. Father told me last night that it is one hundred and eight feet high, fifty feet broad, and has over five thousand pipes; it has sixty-four stops, if you know what they are, I don't, and three key-boards."

"Good for you!" said Ben. "You have a fine memory. My head is a perfect colander for figures; they slip through as fast as they're poured in. But other facts and historical events stay behind—that's some consolation."

"There we differ," returned Van Mounen, "I'm great on names and figures, but history, take it altogether, seems to me to be the most hopeless kind of a jumble."

Meantime Carl and Ludwig were having a discussion concerning some square wooden monuments they had observed in the interior of the church; Ludwig declared that each bore the name of the person buried beneath, and Carl insisted that they had no names, but only the heraldic arms of the deceased painted on a black ground, with the date of the death in gilt letters.

"I ought to know," said Carl, "for I walked across to the east side, to look for the cannon-ball which mother told me was embedded there. It was fired

into the church, in the year fifteen hundred and
something, by those rascally Spaniards, while the
services were going on. There it was in the wall,
sure enough, and while I was walking back, I noticed
the monuments—I tell you, they haven't a sign of
a name upon them."

"Ask Peter," said Ludwig, only half convinced.

"Carl is right," replied Peter, who, though con-
versing with Jacob, had overheard their dispute.
"Well, Jacob, as I was saying, Handel, the great com-
poser, chanced to visit Haarlem and of course he at
once hunted up this famous organ. He gained admit-
tance, and was playing upon it with all his might,
when the regular organist chanced to enter the building. The man stood awestruck; he was a good player himself, but he had never heard such music before. 'Who is there?' he cried, 'If it is not an angel
or the devil, it must be Handel!' When he discovered that it was the great musicion, he was still
more mystified! 'But how is this?' said he, 'you
have done impossible things—no ten fingers on earth
can play the passages you have given; human hands
couldn't control all the keys and stops!' 'I know it;'
said Handel, cooly, 'and for that reason, I was forced
to strike some notes with the end of my nose.' Donder! just think how the old organist must have
stared!"

"Hey! What?" exclaimed Jacob, startled when
Peter's animated voice suddenly became silent.

"Haven't you heard me, you rascal?" was the indignant rejoinder.

"Oh, yes—no—the fact is—I heard you at first—
I'm awake now, but I do believe I've been walking
beside you half asleep," stammered Jacob, with such
a doleful bewildered look on his face, that Peter
could not help laughing.

CHAPTER XIV

THE MAN WITH FOUR HEADS

After leaving the church, the boys stopped near
by in the open market-place, to look at the bronze
statue of Laurens Janzoon Coster, who is believed
by the Dutch to have been the inventor of printing.
This is disputed by those who award the same honor
to Johannes Gutenberg of Mayence; while many
maintain that Faustus, a servant of Coster, stole his
master's wooden types on a Christmas eve, when
the latter was at church, and fled with his booty,
and his secret, to Mayence. Coster was a native of
Haarlem, and the Hollanders are naturally anxious
to secure the credit of the invention for their illus-
trious townsman. Certain it is, that the first book
he printed, is kept, by the city, in a silver case wrap-
ped in silk, and is shown with great caution as a
most precious relic. It is said he first conceived
the idea of printing from cutting his name upon the
bark of a tree, and afterwards pressing a piece of
paper upon the characters.

Of course Lambert and his English friend fullly
discussed this subject. They also had rather a warm
argument concerning another invention. Lambert
declared that the honor of giving both the telescope
and miscroscope to the world lay between Metius
and Jansen, both Hollanders; while Ben as stoutly
insisted that Roger Bacon, an English monk of the
thirteenth century, "wrote out the whole thing, sir,
perfect descriptions of microscopes and telescopes,
too, long before either of those other fellows were
born."

On one subject, however, they both agreed: that
the art of curing and pickling herrings was discov-

ered by William Beukles of Holland, and that the
country did perfectly right in honoring him as a na-
tional benefactor, for its wealth and importance had
been in a great measure due to its herring trade.

"It is astonishing," said Ben, "in what prodigious
quantities those fish are found. I don't know how it
is here, but on the coast of England, off Yarmouth,
the herring shoals have been known to be six and
seven feet deep with fish."

"That is prodigious, indeed," said Lambert, "but
you know your word herring is derived from the
German heer, an army, on account of a way the fish
have of coming in large numbers."

"We propose to move on," said Van Holp, "there
is nothing to see at this season in the Bosch—the
Bosch is a noble wood, Benjamin, a grand Park
where they have most magnificent trees, protected
by law—Do you understand?"

"Ya!" nodded Ben, as the Captain proceeded.

"Unless you all desire to visit the Museum of Nat-
ural History, we may go on the grand canal again.
If we had more time it would be pleasant to take
Benjamin up the Blue Stairs."

"What are the Blue Stairs, Lambert?" asked Ben.

"They are the highest point of the Dunes. You
have a grand view of the ocean from there, besides
a fine chance to see how wonderful these Dunes are.
One can hardly believe that the wind could ever heap
up sand in so remarkable a way. But we have to go
through Bloemendal to get there—not a very pretty
village, and some distance from here. What do you
say?"

"Oh, I am ready for anything. For my part, I
would rather steer direct for Leyden, but we'll do
as the Captain says—hey, Jacob?"

"Ya, dat ish goot," said Jacob, who felt decidedly

more like taking another nap than ascending the Blue Stairs.

The captain was in favor of going to Leyden.

"It's four long miles from here. Full sixteen of your English miles, Benjamin. We have no time to lose if you wish to reach there before midnight. Decide quickly, boys—Blue Stairs or Leyden?"

"Leyden," they answered—and were out of Haarlem in a twinkling, admiring the lofty, tower-like windmills and pretty country-seats as they left the city behind them.

"If you really wish to see Haarlem," said Lambert to Ben, after they had skated awhile in silence, "you should visit it in summer. It is the greatest place in the world for beautiful flowers. The walks around the city are superb; and the 'Wood' with its miles of noble elms, all in full feather, is something to remember. You need not smile, old fellow, at my saying 'full feather'—I was thinking of waving plumes, and got my words mixed up a little. But a Dutch elm beats everything; it is the noblest tree on earth, Ben—if you except the English oak—"

"Aye," said Ben, solemnly, "if you except the English oak—" and for some moments he could scarcely see the canal because Robby and Jenny kept bobbing in the air before his eyes.

CHAPTER XV

FRIENDS IN NEED

Meantime, the other boys were listening to Peter's account of an incident which had long ago occurred in a part of the city where stood an ancient castle, whose lord had tyrannized over the burghers of the town to such an extent, that they surrounded his castle, and laid siege to it. Just at the last extremity, when the haughty lord felt that he could hold out no longer, and was preparing to sell his life as dearly as possible, his lady appeared on the ramparts, and offered to surrender everything, provided she was permitted to bring out, and retain, as much of her precious household goods as she could carry upon her back. The promise was given—and forth came the lady from the gate-way, bearing her husband upon her shoulders. The burghers' pledge preserved him from the fury of the troops, but left them free to wreak their vengeance upon the castle.

"Do you believe that story, Captain Peter?" asked Carl, in an incredulous tone.

"Of course, I do; it is historical. Why should I doubt it?"

"Simply because no woman could do it—and, if she could, she wouldn't. That is my opinion."

"And I believe there are many who would.—That is, to save any one they really cared for," said Ludwig.

Jacob, who in spite of his fat and sleepiness, was of rather a sentimental turn, had listened with deep interest.

"That is right, little fellow," he said, nodding his head approvingly, "I believe every word of it. I

shall never marry a woman who would not be glad
to do as much for me."

"Heaven help her!" cried Carl, turning to gaze
at the speaker, "why, Poot, three men couldn't do
it!"

"Perhaps not," said Jacob quietly—feeling that he
had asked rather too much of the future Mrs. Poot.
"But she must be willing, that is all."

"Aye," responded Peter's cheery voice, "willing
heart makes nimble foot—and who knows, but it
may make strong arms also."

"Pete," asked Ludwig, changing the subject, "did
you tell me last night that the painter Wouvermans
was born in Haarlem?"

"Yes, and Jacob Ruysdael and Berghem too. I
like Berghem because he was always good-natured—
they say he always sang while he painted, and
though he died nearly two hundred years ago, there
are traditions still afloat concerning his pleasant
laugh. He was a great painter and he had a wife
as cross as Xantippe."

"They balanced each other finely," said Ludwig,
"he was kind and she was cross. But, Peter, before
I forget it, wasn't that picture of St. Hubert and
the Horse painted by Wouvermans? You remember
father showed us an engraving from it last night."

"Yes, indeed; there is a story connected with that
picture."

"Tell us!" cried two or three, drawing closer to
Peter as they skated on.

"Wouvermans," began the captain, oratorically,
"was born in 1620, just four years before Berghem.
He was a master of his art, and especially excelled
in painting horses. Strange as it may seem, people
were so long finding out his merits, that, even after
he had arrived at the height of his excellence, he was

obliged to sell his pictures for very paltry prices.
The poor artist became completely discouraged, and,
worse, than all, was over head and ears in debt. One
day he was talking over his troubles with his father-
confessor, who was one of the few who recognized
his genius. The priest determined to assist him, and
accordingly lent him six hundred guilders, advising
him at the same time to demand a better price for
his pictures. Wouvermans did so, and in the meantime paid his debts. Matters brightened with him
at once. Everybody appreciated the great artist
who painted such costly pictures. He grew rich.
The six hundred guilders were returned, and in
gratitude, Wouvermans sent also a work which he
had painted, representing his benefactor as Saint
Hubert kneeling before his horse—the very picture,
Ludwig, of which we were speaking last night."

"So! so!" exclaimed Ludwig, with deep interest,
"I must take another look at the engraving as soon
as we get home."

At that same hour, while Ben was skating with
his companions beside the Holland dike, Robby and
Jenny stood in their pretty English school-house,
ready to join in the duties of their reading class.

"Commence! Master Robert Dobbs," said the
teacher, "page 242, now, sir, mind every stop."

And Robby, in a quick childish voice, roared forth
at school-room pitch:

"Lessen 62.—The Hero of Haarlem

"Many years ago, there lived in Haarlem, one of
the principal cities of Holland, a sunny-haired boy,
of gentle disposition. His father was a sluicer, that
is, a man whose business it was to open and close
the sluices, or large oaken gates, that are placed at
regular distances across the entrances of the canal,

to regulate the amount of water that shall flow into them.

"The sluicer raises the gates more or less according to the quantity of water required, and closes them carefully at night, in order to avoid all possible danger of an over supply running into the canal, or the water would soon overflow it and inundate the surrounding country. As a great portion of Holland is lower than the level of the sea, the waters are kept from flooding the land, only by means of strong dikes, or barriers, and by means of these sluices, which are often strained to the utmost by the pressure of the rising tides. Even the little children in Holland know that constant watchfulness is required to keep the rivers and ocean from overwhelming the country, and that a moment's neglect of the sluicer's duty may bring ruin and death to all."

"[Very good," said the teacher; "now, Susan."]

"One lovely autumn afternoon, when the boy was about eight years old, he obtained his parents' consent to carry some cakes to a blind man who lived out in the country, on the other side of the dike. The little fellow started on his errand with a light heart, and having spent an hour with his grateful old friend, he bade him farewell and started on his homeward walk.

"Trudging stoutly along by the canal, he noticed how the autumn rains had swollen the waters. Even while humming his careless, childish song, he thought of his father's brave old gates and felt glad of their strength, for, thought he, 'if they gave way, where would father and mother be? These pretty fields would be all covered with the angry waters— father always calls them the angry waters, I suppose he thinks they are mad at him for keeping them

out so long.' And with these thoughts just flitting
across his brain, the little fellow stooped to pick the
pretty blue flowers that grew along his way. Sometimes he stopped to throw some feathery seed-ball
in the air, and watch it as it floated away; sometimes he listened to the stealthy rustling of a rabbit,
speeding through the grass, but oftener he smiled as
he recalled the happy light he had seen arise on the
weary, listening face of his blind old friend."

["Now, Henry," said the teacher, nodding to the
next little reader.]

"Suddenly the boy looked around him in dismay.
He had not noticed that the sun was setting; now he
saw that his long shadow on the grass had vanished.
It was growing dark, he was still some distance
from home, and in a lonely ravine, where even the
blue flowers had turned to gray. He quickened his
footsteps; and with a beating heart recalled many a
nursery tale of children belated in dreary forests.
Just as he was bracing himself for a run, he was
startled by the sound of trickling water. Whence
did it come? He looked up and saw a small hole in
the dike through which a tiny stream was flowing.
Any child in Holland will shudder at the thought of
a leak in the dike! The boy understood the danger
at a glance. That little hole, if the water were allowed to trickle through would soon be a large one,
and a terrible inundation would be the result.

"Quick as a flash, he saw his duty. Throwing
away his flowers, the boy clambered up the heights,
until he reached the hole. His chubby little finger
was thrust in, almost before he knew it. The flowing
was stopped! 'Ah!' he thought, with a chuckle of
boyish delight, 'the angry waters must stay back
now. Haarlem shall not be drowned while I am
here!'

"This was all very well at first, but the night was falling rapidly; chill vapors filled the air. Our little hero began to tremble with cold and dread. He shouted loudly; he screamed 'Come here! come here!' but no one came. The cold grew more intense, a numbness, commencing in the tired little finger, crept over his hand and arm, and soon his whole body was filled with pain. He shouted again, 'Will no one come? Mother! mother!' Alas, his mother, good practical soul, had already locked the doors, and had fully resolved to scold him on the morrow for spending the night with blind Jansen without her permission. He tried to whistle, perhaps some straggling boy might heed the signal; but his teeth chattered so, it was impossible. Then he called on God for help; and the answer came, through a holy resolution—'I will stay here till to-morrow.'"

["Now, Jenny Dobbs," said the teacher. Jenny's eyes were glistering, but she took a long breath and commenced:]

"The midnight moon looked down upon that small solitary form, sitting upon a stone, half-way up the dike. His head was bent, but he was not asleep, for every now and then one restless hand rubbed feebly the outstretched arm that seemed fastened to the dike—and often the pale, tearful face turned quickly at some real or fancied sound.

"How can we know the sufferings of that long and fearful watch—what falterings of purpose, what childish terrors came over the boy as he thought of the warm little bed at home, of his parents, his brothers and sisters, then looked into the cold, dreary night! If he drew away that tiny finger, the angry waters, grown angrier still, would rush forth, and never stop until they had swept over the town. No, he would hold it there till daylight—if he lived! He was not very sure of living. What did this strange buzzing mean? and then the knives that seemed pricking and piercing him from head to foot? He was not certain now that he could draw his finger away, even if he wished to.

At daybreak a clergyman, returning from the bedside of a sick parishioner, thought he heard groans as he walked along on the top of the dike. Bending, he saw, far down on the side, a child apparently writhing with pain.

"In the name of wonder, boy," he exclaimed, "what are you doing there?"

"I am keeping the water from running out," was the simple answer of the little hero. "Tell them to come quick."

It is needless to add that they did come quickly and that—

["Jenny Dobbs," said the teacher, rather impatiently, "if you cannot control your feelings so as to read distinctly, we will wait until you recover yourself."

"Yes, sir!" said Jenny, quite startled.]

It was strange; but at that very moment, Ben, far over the sea, was saying to Lambert—

"The noble little fellow! I have frequently met with an account of the incident, but I never knew, till now, that it was really true."

"True! Of course it is," said Lambert, kindling. "I have given you the story just as mother told it to me, years ago. Why, there is not a child in Holland who does not know it. And, Ben, you may not think so, but that little boy represents the spirit of the whole country. Not a leak can show itself anywhere either in its politics, honor, or public safety, that a million fingers are not ready to stop it, at any cost."

"Whew!" cried Master Ben, "big talking that!"

"It's true talk anyway," rejoined Lambert, so very quietly that Ben wisely resolved to make no further comment.

CHAPTER XVI

ON THE CANAL

The skating season had commenced unusually early; our boys were by no means alone upon the ice. The afternoon was so fine, that men, women, and children, bent upon enjoying the holiday, had flocked to the grand canal from far and near. Saint Nicholas had evidently remembered the favorite pastime; shining new skates were everywhere to be seen. Whole families were skimming their way to Haarlem or Leyden or the neighboring villages. The ice seemed fairly alive. Men noticed the erect, easy carriage of the women, and their picturesque variety of costume. There were the latest fashions fresh from Paris, floating past dingy, moth-eaten garments that had seen service through two generations; coal-scuttle bonnets perched over freckled faces bright with holiday smiles; stiff muslin caps, with wings at the sides, flapping beside cheeks rosy with health and contentment; furs, too, encircling the whitest of throats; and scanty garments fluttering below faces ruddy with exercise—In short every quaint and comical mixture of dry-goods and flesh that Holland could furnish, seemed sent to enliven the scene.

There were belles from Leyden, and fishwives from the border villages; cheese women from Gouda, and prim matrons from beautiful country-seats on the Haarlemmer Meer. Gray-headed skaters were constantly to be seen; wrinkled old women, with baskets upon their heads; and plump little toddlers on skates clutching at their mother's gowns. Some women carried their babies upon their backs, firmly secured with a bright shawl. The effect was pretty

and graceful as they darted by, or sailed slowly past,
now nodding to an acquaintance, now chirruping
and throwing soft baby-talk to the muffled little
ones they carried.

Boys and girls were chasing each other, and hid-
behind the one-horse sleds, that, loaded high with
peat or timber, pursued their cautious way along the
track marked out as "safe." Beautiful, queenly
women were there, enjoyment sparkling in their
quiet eyes. Sometimes a long file of young men,
each grasping the coat of the one before him, flew
by with electric speed; and sometimes the ice
squeaked under the chair of some gorgeous old dow-
ager, or rich burgomaster's lady—who, very red in
the nose, and sharp in the eyes, looked like a scare-
thaw invented by old father Winter for the protection of his skating grounds. The chair would be
heavy with footstoves and cushions, to say nothing
of the old lady. Mounted upon shining runners it
slid along, pushed by the sleepiest of servants, who,
looking neither to the right nor the left, bent himself to his task while she cast direful glances upon
the screaming little rowdies who invariably acted
as body-guard.

As for the men, they were pictures of placid enjoyment. Some were attired in ordinary citizen's
dress; but many looked odd enough with their short
woolen coats, wide breeches, and big silver buckles.
These seemed to Ben like little boys who had, by a
miracle, sprung suddenly into manhood, and were
forced to wear garments that their astonished mothers had altered in a hurry. He noticed, too, that
nearly all the men had pipes, as they passed him
whizzing and smoking like so many locomotives.
There was every variety of pipes from those of common clay to the most expensive meerschaums mount-

ed in silver and gold. Some were carved into extraordinary and fantastic shapes, representing birds,
flowers, heads, bugs, and dozens of other things;
some resembled the "Dutchman's pipe" that grows
in our American woods; some were red, and many
were of a pure snowy white; but the most respectable were those which were ripening into a shaded
brown—The deeper and richer the brown, of course
the more honored the pipe, for it was a proof that
the owner, if honestly shading it, was deliberately
devoting his manhood to the effort—What pipe
would not be proud to be the object of such a sacrifice!

For awhile, Ben skated on in silence. There was
so much to engage his attention that he almost forgot his companions. Part of the time he had been
watching the ice-boats as they flew over the great
Haarlemmer Meer (or Lake), the frozen surface of
which was now plainly visible from the canal. These
boats had very large sails, much larger in proportion, than those of ordinary vessels, and were set
upon a triangular frame furnished with an iron
"runner" at each corner,—the widest part of the
triangle crossing the bow, and its point stretching
beyond the stern. They had rudders for guiding,
and brakes for arresting their progress; and were
of all sizes and kinds, from small, rough affairs managed by a boy, to large and beautiful ones filled with
gay pleasure parties, and manned by competent
sailors, who, smoking their stumpy pipes, reefed and
tacked and steered with great solemnity and pre-
cision.

Some of the boats were painted and gilded in
gaudy style and flaunted gay pennons from their
mast-heads; others white as snow, with every spot-
less sail rounded by the wind looked like swans

borne onward by a resistless current. It seemed to
Ben as, following his fancy, he watched one of these
in the distance, that he could almost hear its helpless, terrified cry, but he soon found that the sound
arose from a nearer and less romantic cause—from
an ice-boat not fifty yards from him, using its brakes
to avoid a collision with a peat-sled.

It was a rare thing for these boats to be upon the
canal and their appearance generally caused no little
ercitement among skaters, especially among the
timid; but to-day every ice-boat in the country seemed afloat or rather aslide, and the canal had its full
share.

Ben, though delighted at the sight, was often
startled at the swift approach of the resistless, high-
winged things threatening to dart in any and every
possible direction. It required all his energies to
keep out of the way of the passers-by, and to prevent
those screaming little urchins from upsetting him
with their sleds. Once he halted to watch some boys
who were making a hole in the ice preparatory
to using their fishing spears. Just as he concluded
to start again, he found himself suddenly bumped
into an old lady's lap. Her push-chair had come
upon him from the rear. The old lady screamed, the
servant who was propelling her gave a warning hiss
—In another instant Ben found himself apologizing
to empty air; the indignant old lady was far ahead.

This was a slight mishap compared with one that
now threatened him. A huge ice-boat, under full
sail, came tearing down the canal, almost paralyz-
ing Ben with the thought of instant destruction. It
was close upon him! He saw its gilded prow, heard
the schipper shout, felt the great boom fairly whizz
over his head, was blind, deaf and dumb all in an instant, then opened his eyes, to find himself spinning

some yards behind its great, skate-like rudder. It
had passed within an inch of his shoulder, but he
was safe! safe to see England again, safe to kiss
the dear faces that for an instant had flashed before
him one by one—father, mother, Robby and Jenny—
that great boom had dashed their images into his
very soul. He knew now how much he loved them.
Perhaps this knowledge made him face complacently
the scowls of those on the canal who seemed to feel
that a boy in danger was necessarily a bad boy need-
ing instant reprimand.

Lambert chided him roundly.

"I thought it was all over with you, you careless
fellow! Why don't you look where you are going.
Not content with sitting on all the old ladies' laps,
you must make a Juggernaut of every ice-boat that
comes along. We shall have to hand you over to the
aanspreekers yet, if you don't look out!"

"Please don't," said Ben, with mock humility—
then seeing how pale Lambert's lips were, added in
a low tone:

"I do believe I thought more in that one moment,
Van Mounen, than in all the rest of my past life."

There was no reply, and, for awhile, the two boys
skated on in silence.

Soon a faint sound of distant bells reached their
ears.

"Hark!" said Ben, "what is that?"

"The carillons," replied Lambert. "They are trying the bells in the chapel of yonder village. Ah!
Ben, you should hear the chimes of the 'New Church'
at Delft; they are superb—nearly five hundred
sweet-toned bells, and one of the best carilloneurs
of Holland to play upon them. Hard work, though;
they say the fellow often has to go to bed from posi-
tive exhaustion, after his performances. You see,

the bells are attached to a kind of keyboard, something like they have on piano-fortes; there are also a set of pedals for the feet; when a brisk tune is going on, the player looks like a kicking frog fastened to his seat with a skewer."

"For shame," said Ben, indignantly.

Peter had, for the present, exhausted his stock of Haarlem anecdotes, and now, having nothing to do but to skate, he and his three companions were hastening to "catch up" with Lambert and Ben.

"That English lad is fleet enough," said Peter, "if he were a born Hollander he could do no better. Generally these John Bulls make but a sorry figure on skates—Hollo! Here you are, Van Mounen, why we hardly hoped for the honor of meeting you again. Who were you flying from in such haste?"

"Snails," retorted Lambert. "What kept you?"

"We have been talking—and, besides, we halted once to give Poot a chance to rest."

"He begins to look rather worn out," said Lambert in a low voice.

Just then a beautiful ice-boat with reefed sail, and flying streamers, swept leisurely by. Its deck was filled with children muffled up to their chins. Looking at them from the ice you could see only smiling little faces imbedded in bright-colored, woolen wrappings. They were singing a chorus in honor of Saint Nicholas. The music, starting in the discord of a hundred childish voices, floated, as it rose, into exquisite harmony:

Friend of sailors, and of children!
  Double claim have we,
As in youthful joy we're sailing,
  O'er a frozen sea!
        Nicholas! Saint Nicholas!
        Let us sing to thee.

While through Wintry air we're rushing,
　　As our voices blend,
Are you near us?　Do you hear us,
　　Nicholas, our friend?
　　　　　　　　Nicholas!　Saint Nicholas!
　　　　　　　　Love can never end.

Sunny sparkles, bright before us,
　　Chase away the cold!
Hearts where sunny thoughts are welcome,
　　Never can grow old—
　　　　　　　　Nicholas! Saint Nicholas—
　　　　　　　　Never can grow old!

Pretty gift and loving lesson,
　　Festival and glee,
Bid us thank thee as we're sailing
　　O'er the frozen sea—
　　　　　　　　Nicholas!　Saint Nicholas!
　　　　　　　　So we sing to thee!

CHAPTER XVII

JACOB POOT CHANGES THE PLAN

The last note died away in the distance. Our boys, who in their vain efforts to keep up with the boat, had felt that they were skating backward, turned to look at one another.

"How beautiful that was!" exclaimed Van Mounen.

"Just like a dream!" said Ludwig.

Jacob drew close to Ben, giving his usual approving nod, as he spoke:

"Dat ish goot. Dat ish te pest vay—I shay petter to take to Leyden mit a poat!"

"Take a boat!" exclaimed Ben, in dismay—"why, man, our plan was to skate, not to be carried like little children—"

"Tuyfels!" retorted Jacob, "dat ish no little—no papies—to go for poat!"

The boys laughed, but exchanged uneasy glances. It would be great fun to jump on an ice-boat, if they had a chance; but to abandon so shamefully their grand undertaking—Who could think of such a thing?

An animated discussion arose at once.

Captain Peter brought his party to a halt.

"Boys," said he, "it strikes me that we should consult Jacob's wishes in this matter. He started the excursion, you know."

"Pooh!" sneered Carl, throwing a contemptuous glance at Jacob, "who's tired? We can rest all night at Leyden."

Ludwig and Lambert looked anxious and disappointed. It was no slight thing to lose the credit of having skated all the way from Broek to the Hague, and back again; but both agreed that Jacob should decide the question.

Good-natured, tired Jacob! He read the popular sentiment at a glance.

"Oh! no," he said, in Dutch. "I was joking. We will skate, of course."

The boys gave a delighted shout, and started on again with renewed vigor—

All but Jacob. He tried his best not to seem fatigued, and, by not saying a word, saved his breath and energy for the great business of skating. But in vain. Before long, the stout body grew heavier and heavier—the tottering limbs weaker and weaker. Worse than all, the blood, anxious to get as far as possible from the ice, mounted to the puffy, good-natured cheeks, and made the roots of his thin, yellow hair glow into a fiery red.

This kind of work is apt to summon Vertigo, of whom good Hans Andersen writes—the same who hurls daring young hunters from the mountains, or spins them from the sharpest heights of the glaciers, or catches them as they tread the stepping stones of the mountains torrent.

Vertigo came, unseen, to Jacob. After tormenting him awhile, with one touch sending a chill from head to foot, with the next, scorching every vein with fever, she made the canal rock and tremble beneath him, the white sails bow and spin as they passed, then cast him heavily upon the ice.

"Hallo!" cried Van Mounen. "There goes Poot!"

Ben sprang hastily forward.

"Jacob! Jacob, are you hurt?"

Peter and Carl were lifting him. The face was white enough now. It seemed like a dead face—even the good-natured look was gone.

A crowd collected. Peter unbuttoned the poor

boy's jacket, loosened his red tippet, and blew between the parted lips.

"Stand off, good people!" he cried, "give him air!"

"Lay him down," called out a woman from the crowd.

"Stand him upon his feet," shouted another.

"Give him wine," growled a stout fellow who was driving a loaded sled.

"Yes! yes, give him wine!" echoed everybody.

Ludwig and Lambert shouted in concert:

"Wine! wine! Who has wine!"

A sleepy-eyed Dutchman began to fumble mysteriously under the heaviest of blue jackets, saying as he did so:

"Not so much noise, young masters, not so much noise. The boy was a fool to faint off like a girl!"

"Wine, quick!" cried Peter, who. with Ben's help, was rubbing Jacob from head to foot.

Ludwig stretched forth his hand imploringly toward the Dutchman, who with an air of great importance was still fumbling beneath the jacket.

"Do hurry! He will die! Has any one else any wine?"

"He is dead!" said an awful voice from among the bystanders.

This startled the Dutchman.

"Have a care!" he said, reluctantly drawing forth a small blue flask, "this is schnaps. A little is enough."

A little was enough. The paleness gave way to a faint flush. Jacob opened his eyes, and—half bewildered, half ashamed,—feebly tried to free himself from those who were supporting him.

There was no alternative, now, for our party but to have their exhausted comrade carried, in some way, to Leyden. As for expecting him to skate any more that day, the thing was impossible. In truth, by this time each boy began to entertain secret yearnings towards ice-boats, and to avow a Spartan resolve not to desert Jacob. Fortunately a gentle, steady breeze was setting southward. If some accommodating skipper would but come along, matters would not be quite so bad after all.

Peter hailed the first sail that appeared; the men in the stern would not even look at him. Three drays on runners came along, but they were already loaded to the utmost. Then an ice-boat, a beautiful, tempting little one, whizzed past like an arrow. The boys had just time to stare eagerly at it when it was gone. In despair, they resolved to prop up Jacob with their strong arms as well as they could, and take him to the nearest village.

At that moment a very shabby ice-boat came in sight. With but little hope of success, Peter hailed it, at the same time taking off his hat and flourishing it in the air.

The sail was lowered, then came the scraping sound of the brake, and a pleasant voice called out from the deck:

"What now?"

"Will you take us on?" cried Peter, hurrying with his companions as fast as he could, for the boat was "bringing to" some distance ahead, "will you take us on?"

"We'll pay for the ride!" shouted Carl.

The man on board scarcely noticed him except to mutter something about its not being a trekschuit. Still looking toward Peter he asked:

"How many?"

"Six."

"Well, it's Nicholas' day—up with you! Young gentleman sick?" (nodding towards Jacob.)

"Yes—broken down—skated all the way from Broek," answered Peter—"Do you go to Leyden?"

"That's as the wind says—it's blowing that way now—scramble up!"

Poor Jacob! if that willing Mrs. Poot had only appeared just then, her services would have been invaluable. It was as much as the boys could do to hoist him into the boat. All were in at last. The schipper, puffing away at his pipe, let out the sail, lifted the brake, and sat in the stern with folded arms.

"Whew! How fast we go!" cried Ben, "this is something like. Feel better, Jacob?"

"Much petter I tanks you."

"Oh, you'll be as good as new in ten minutes. This makes a fellow feel like a bird."

Jacob nooded, and blinked his eyes.

"Don't go to sleep, Jacob; it's too cold. You might never wake up you know. Persons often freeze to death in that way."

"I no sleep," said Jacob confidently—and in two minutes he was snoring.

Carl and Ludwig laughed.

"We must wake him!" cried Ben, "it is dangerous, I tell you—Jacob! Ja-ac—"

Captain Peter interfered, for three of the boys were helping Ben for the fun of the thing.

"Nonsense! don't shake him! Let him alone, boys. One never snores like that when one's freezing. Cover him up with something. Here, this cloak will do; hey, schipper?" and he looked toward the stern for permission to use it.

The man nodded.

"There," said Peter, tenderly adjusting the garment, "let him sleep. He will be frisky as a lamb when he awakes. How far are we from Leyden, schipper?"

"Not more'n a couple of pipes," replied a voice, rising from smoke like the genii in fairy tales (puff! puff!), "likely not more'n one an' a half (puff! puff!) if this wind holds!" (puff! puff! puff!).

"What is the man saying, Lambert?" asked Ben, who was holding his mittened hands against his cheeks to ward off the cutting air.

"He says we're about two pipes from Leyden. Half the boors here on the canal measure distances by the time it takes them to finish a pipe."

"How ridiculous."

"See here, Benjamin Dobbs," retorted Lambert, growing unaccountably indignant at Ben's quiet smile; "see here, you've a way of calling every other thing you see on this side of the German ocean, 'ridiculous'. It may suit you this word; but it don't suit me. When you want anything ridiculous just remember your English custom of making the Lord Mayor of London, at his installation, count the nails in a horseshoe to prove his learning."

"Who told you we had any such custom as that?" cried Ben, looking grave in an instant.

"Why, I know it, no use of any one telling me. It's in all the books—and it's true. It strikes me," continued Lambert, laughing in spite of himself, "that you have been kept in happy ignorance of a good many ridiculous things on your side of the map."

"Humph!" exclaimed Ben, trying not to smile. "I'll inquire into that Lord Mayor business when I get home. There must be some mistake. B-r-r-oooo! how fast we're going. This is glorious!"

It was a grand sail, or ride, I scarcely know which to call it; perhaps "fly" would be the best word; for

the boys felt very much as Sinbad did when, tied to
the roc's leg, he darted through the clouds; or as
Bellerophon felt when he shot through the air on the
back of his winged horse Pegasus. Sailing, riding,
or flying, whichever it was, everything was rushing
past, backward—and, before they had time to draw
a long breath, Leyden itself, with its high peaked-
roofs, flew half-way to meet them.

When the city came in sight it was high time to
waken the sleeper. That feat accomplished, Peter's
prophecy came to pass. Master Jacob was quite restored and in excellent spirits.

The schipper made a feeble remonstrance when
Peter, with hearty thanks, endeavored to slip some
silver pieces into his tough, brown palm.

"Ye see, young master," said he, drawing away
his hand, "the regular line o' trade's one thing, and
a favor's another."

"I know it," said Peter, "but those boys and girls
of yours will want sweets when you get home. Buy
them some in the name of Saint Nicholas."

The man grinned. "Aye, true enough, I've young
'uns in plenty, a clean boat-load of them. You are
a sharp young master at guessing."

This time, the knotty hand hitched forward again,
quite carelessly, it seemed, but its palm was upward.
Peter hastily dropped in the money and moved away.

The sail soon came tumbling down. Scrape,
scrape went the brake, scattering an ice shower
round the boat.

"Good-by, schipper!" shouted the boys, seizing
their skates and leaping from the deck one by one,
"many thanks to you!"

"Good-by! good-b— Hold! here! stop! I want
my coat."

Ben was carefully assisting his cousin over the side of the boat.

"What is the man shouting about. Oh, I know, you have his wrapper round your shoulders!"

"Dat ish true," answered Jacob, half jumping, half tumbling down upon the frame work, "dat ish vot make him sho heavy."

"Made you so heavy, you mean, Poot?"

"Ya, made you so heavy—dat ish true," said Jacob innocently, as he worked himself free from the big wrapper, "dere, now you hands it mit him, straits way and tells him I vos much tanks for dat."

"Ho! for an inn!" cried Peter, as they stepped into the city. "Be brisk, my fine fellows!"

CHAPTER XVIII

MYNHEER KLEEF AND HIS BILL OF FARE

The boys soon found an unpretending establishment near the Breedstraat (Broad Street) with a funnily painted lion over the door. This was the Roode Leeuw or Red Lion, kept by one Huygens Kleef, a stout Dutchman with short legs and a very long pipe.

By this time they were in a ravenous condition. The tiffin, taken at Haarlem, had served only to give them an appetite, and this had been heightened by their exercise, and swift sail upon the canal.

"Come, mine host! give us what you can!" cried Peter rather pompously.

"I can give you anything—everything," answered Mynheer Kleef, performing a difficult bow.

"Well, give us sausage and pudding."

"Ah, mynheer, the sausage is all gone. There is no pudding."

"Salmagundi, then, and plenty of it."

"That is out also, young master."

"Eggs, and be quick."

"Winter eggs are very poor eating," answered the innkeeper, puckering his lips and lifting his eyebrows.

"No eggs?—well—Caviare."

The Dutchman raised his fat hands:

"Caviare! That is made of gold! Who has caviare to sell?"

Peter had sometimes eaten it at home; he knew

that it was made of the roes of the sturgeon, and certain other large fish, but he had no idea of its cost.

"Well, mine host, what have you?"

"What have I? Everything. I have rye-bread,
sour-krout, potato-salad and the fattest herring in
Leyden."

"What do you say, boys?" asked the captain, "will
that do?"

"Yes," cried the famished youths, "if he'll only be
quick."

Mynheer moved off like one walking in his sleep,
but soon opened his eyes wide at the miraculous
manner in which his herring were made to disap-
pear. Next came, or rather went, potato-salad, rye-
bread and coffee—then Utrecht water flavored with
orange, and, finally slices of dry ginger-bread. This
last delicacy was not on the regular bill of fare; but
Mynheer Kleef, driven to extremes, solemnly pro-
duced it from his own private stores, and gave only
a placid blink when his voracious young travelers
started up, declaring they had eaten enough.

"I should think so!" he exclaimed internally, but
his smooth face gave no sign.

Softly rubbing his hands, he asked:

"Will your worships have beds?"

"Will your worships have beds?" mocked Carl—
"what do you mean? Do we look sleepy?"

"Not at all, master; but I would cause them to be
warmed and aired. None sleep under damp sheets
at the Red Lion."

"Ah, I understand. Shall we come back here to
sleep, Captain?"

Peter was accustomed to finer lodgings; but this
was a frolic.

"Why not?" he replied, "we can fare excellently here."

"Your worship speaks only the truth," said mynheer with great deference.

"How fine to be called 'your worship'," laughed Ludwig aside to Lambert, while Peter replied:

"Well, mine host, you may get the rooms ready by nine."

"I have one beautiul chamber, with three beds, that will hold all of your worships," said Mynheer Kleef coaxingly.

"That will do."

"Whew!" whistled Carl when they reached the street.

Ludwig started. "What now?"

"Nothing—only Mynheer Kleef of the Red Lion little thinks how we shall make things spin in that same room to-night—We'll set the bolsters flying!"

"Order!" cried the captain. "Now, boys, I must seek this great Doctor Boekman before I sleep. If he is in Leyden it will be no great task to find him, for he always puts up at the Golden Eagle when he comes here. I wonder that you did not all go to bed at once—still, as you are awake, what say you to walking with Ben up by the Museum or the Stadhuis?"

"Agreed," said Ludwig and Lambert; but Jacob preferred to go with Peter. In vain Ben tried to persuade him to remain at the Inn and rest. He declared that he never felt "petter," and wished of all things to take a look at the city, for it was his first "stop mit Leyden."

"Oh, it will not harm him," said Lambert. "How long the day has been—and what glorious sport we have had. It hardly seems possible that we left Broek only this morning."

Jacob yawned.

"I have enjoyed it well," he said, "but it seems to me at least a week since we started."

Carl laughed, and muttered something about "twenty naps—"

"Here we are at the corner; remember, we all meet at the Red Lion at eight," said the captain, as he and Jacob walked away.

CHAPTER XIX

THE RED LION BECOMES DANGEROUS

The boys were glad to find a blazing fire awaiting them upon their return to the "Red Lion." Carl and his party were there first. Soon afterward Peter and Jacob came in. They had inquired in vain concerning Dr. Boekman. All they could ascertain was that he had been seen in Haarlem that morning.

"As for his being in Leyden," the landlord of the Golden Eagle had said to Peter, "the thing is impossible. He always lodges here when in town. By this time there would be a crowd at my door waiting to consult him—Bah! people make such fools of themselves!"

"He is called a great surgeon," said Peter

"Yes, the greatest in Holland. But what of that! What of being the greatest pill-choker and knife-slasher in the world? The man is a bear. Only last month on this very spot, he called me a pig, before three customers."

"No!" exclaimed Peter, trying to look surprised and indignant.

"Yes, master—A PIG," repeated the landlord, puffing at his pipe with an injured air. "Bah! if he did not pay fine prices and bring customers to my house I would sooner see him in the Vleit canal than give him lodgment."

Perhaps mine host felt that he was speaking too openly to a stranger, or it may be he saw a smile lurking in Peter's face, for he added sharply:

"Come, now, what more do you wish? Supper? Beds?"

"No, mynheer, I am but searching for Dr. Boekman."

"Go find him.   He is not in Leyden."

Peter was not to be put off so easily. After receiving a few more rough words, he succeeded in obtaining permission to leave a note for the famous surgeon, or rather, he bought from his amiable landlord the privilege of writing it there, and a promise that it should be promptly delivered when Doctor Boekman arrived.   This accomplished, Peter and Jacob returned to the "Red Lion."

This inn had once been a fine house, the home of a rich burgher; but, having grown old and shabby, it had passed through many hands, until finally it had fallen into the possession of Mynheer Kleef. He was fond of saying as he looked up at its dingy, broken walls—"mend it, and paint it, and there's not a prettier house in Leyden."   It stood six stories high from the street.   The first three were of equal breadth but of various heights, the last three were in the great, high roof, and grew smaller and smaller like a set of double steps until the top one was lost in a point.   The roof was built of short, shining tiles, and the windows, with their little panes seemed to be scattered irregularly over the face of the building, without the slightest attention to outward effect.   But the public room on the ground floor was the landlord's joy and pride.   He never said "mend it, and paint it," there, for everything was in the highest condition of Dutch neatness and order. If you will but open your mind's eye, you may look into the apartment.

Imagine a large, bare room, with a floor that seemed to be made of squares cut out of glazed earthen pie-dishes, first a yellow piece, then a red, until the whole looked like a vast checkerboard. Fancy a dozen high-backed wooden chairs standing around; then a great hollow chimney place all aglow with its blazing fire, reflected a hundred times in the polished steel fire-dogs; a tiled hearth, tiled sides, tiled top, with a Dutch sentence upon it; and over all, high above one's head, a narrow mantelshelf, filled with shining brass candle-sticks, pipe-lighters and tinder-boxes. Then see in one end of the room, three pine tables; in the other, a closet and a deal dresser. The latter is filled with mugs, dishes, pipes, tankards, earthen and glass bottles, and is guarded at one end by a brass-hooped keg standing upon long legs. Everything dim with tobacco smoke, but otherwise clean as soap and sand can make it. Next picture two sleepy, shabby-looking men, in wooden shoes, seated near the glowing fire-place, hugging their knees and smoking short, stumpy pipes; Mynheer Kleef walking softly and heavily about, clad in leather knee breeches, felt shoes, and a green jacket wider than it is long:—then throw a heap of skates in the corner and put six tired, well-dressed boys in various attitudes, upon the wooden chairs, and you will see the coffeeroom of the "Red Lion" just as it appeared at nine o'clock on the evening of Dec. 6th, 184—. For supper, gingerbread again; slices of Dutch sausage; rye-bread sprinkled with anise-seed; pickles; a bottle of Utrecht water, and a pot of very mysterious coffee. The boys were ravenous enough to take all they could get, and pronounce it excellent. Ben made wry faces, but Jacob declared he had never eaten a better meal! After they had laughed and talked awhile, and counted their money by way of settling a discussion that arose concerning their expenses, the captain marched his company off to bed, led on by a greasy pioneer-boy who carried skates and a candlestick instead of an ax.

One of the ill-favored men by the fire had shuffled

towards the dresser, and was ordering a mug of beer, just as Ludwig, who brought up the rear, was stepping from the apartment.

"I don't like that fellow's eye," he whispered to Carl, "he looks like a pirate, or something of that kind."

"Looks like a granny!" answered Carl in sleepy disdain.

Ludwig laughed uneasily.

"Granny or no granny," he whispered, "I tell you he looks like one of those men in the 'voetspoelen'."

"Pooh!" sneered Carl, "I knew it. That picture was too much for you. Look sharp now, and see if yon fellow with the candle doesn't look like the other villain."

"No, indeed, his face is as honest as a Gouda cheese. But, I say, Carl, that really was a horrid picture."

"Humph! Why did you stare at it so long for?"

"I couldn't help it."

By this time the boys had reached the "beautiful room with three beds in it." A dumpy little maiden with long ear-rings met them at the doorway, dropped them a curtsy, and passed out. She carried a long-handled thing that resembled a frying-pan with a cover.

"I am glad to see that," said Van Mounen to Ben. "What?"

"Why, the warming-pan! It's full of hot ashes, she's been heating our beds."

"O! a warming-pan, eh! Much obliged to her, I'm sure," said Ben, too sleepy to make any further comment.

Ludwig, as we have seen, had not quite lost his friskiness; but the other boys, after one or two feeble attempts at pillow-firing, composed themselves for the night with the greatest dignity. Nothing like fatigue for making boys behave themselves.

"Good-night, boys!" said Peter's voice from under the covers.

"Good-night," called back everybody but Jacob, who already lay snoring beside the captain.

"I say," shouted Carl, after a moment, "don't sneeze, anybody. Ludwig's in a fright!"

"No such thing," retorted Ludwig in a smothered voice. Then there was a little whispered dispute, which was ended by Carl saying:

"For my part, I don't know what fear is. But you really are a timid fellow, Ludwig."

Ludwig grunted sleepily, but made no further reply.

It was the middle of the night. The fire had shivered itself to death, and, in place of its gleams, little squares of moonlight lay upon the floor, slowly, slowly shifting their way across the room. Something else was moving also, but they did not see it. Sleeping boys keep but a poor look-out. During the early hours of the night, Jacob Poot had been gradually but surely winding himself with all the bed covers. He now lay like a monster chrysalis beside the half frozen Peter, who, accordingly, was skating with all his might over the coldest, bleakest of dreamland ice-bergs.

Something else, I say, besides the moonlight, was moving across the bare, polished floor—moving not quite so slowly, but quite as stealthily.

Wake up, Ludwig! The voetspoelen pirate is growing real!

No. Ludwig does not waken, but he moans in his sleep.

Does not Carl hear it—Carl the brave, the fearless?

No. Carl is dreaming of the race.

And Jacob? Van Mounen? Ben?

Not they. They, too, are dreaming of the race; and Katrinka is singing through their dreams— laughing, flitting past them; now and then a wave from the great organ surges through their midst.

Still the thing moves, slowly, slowly.

Peter! Captain Peter, there is danger!

Peter heard no call; but, in his dream, he slid a few thousand feet from one ice-berg to another, and the shock awoke him.

Whew! How cold he was! He gave a hopeless, desperate tug at the chrysalis. In vain; sheet, blan- ket and spread were firmly wound about Jacob's inanimate form. Peter looked drowsily toward the window.

"Clear moonlight," he thought, "we shall have pleasant weather to-morrow. Hallo! what's that?"

He saw the moving thing, or rather something black crouching upon the floor, for it had halted as Peter stirred.

He watched in silence.

Soon it moved again, nearer and nearer. It was a man crawling upon hands and feet!

The captain's first impulse was to call out; but he took an instant to consider matters.

The creeper had a shining knife in one hand. This was ugly; but Peter was naturally self-pos- sessed. When the head turned, Peter's eyes were closed as if in sleep; but at other times nothing could be keener, sharper than the captain's gaze.

Closer, closer crept the robber. His back was very near Peter now. The knife was laid softly upon the floor; one careful arm reached forth stealthily to drag the clothes from the chair by the captain's bed—the robbery was commenced.

Now was Peter's time! Holding his breath, he sprang up and leaped with all his strength upon the robber's back, stunning the rascal with the force of the blow. To seize the knife was but a second's work. The robber began to struggle, but Peter sat like a giant astride the prostrate form.

"If you stir," said the brave boy in as terrible a voice as he could command, "stir but one inch, I will plunge this knife into your neck. Boys! Boys! wake up!" he shouted still pressing down the black head, and holding the knife at pricking distance, "give us a hand! I've got him! I've got him!"

The chrysalis rolled over, but made no other sign.

"Up, boys!" cried Peter, never budging, "Ludwig! Lambert! Thunder! Are you all dead?"

Dead! not they. Van Mounen and Ben were on their feet in an instant.

"Hey! What now?" they shouted.

"I've got a robber here," said Peter, coolly. "Lie still, you scoundrel, or I'll slice your head off! Now, boys, cut out your bed cord—plenty of time—he's a dead man if he stirs."

Peter felt that he weighed a thousand pounds. So he did, with that knife in his hand. The man growled and swore, but dared not move.

Ludwig was up, by this time. He had a great jack-knife, the pride of his heart, in his breeches pocket. It could do good service now. They bared the bed-stead in a moment. It was laced backward and forward with a rope.

"I'll cut it," cried Ludwig, sawing away at the knot, "hold him tight, Pete!"

"Never fear!" answered the captain, giving the robber a warning prick.

The boys were soon pulling at the rope like good fellows. It was out at last—a long stout piece.

"Now, boys," commanded the captain, "lift up his rascally arms! Cross his hands over his back! That's right—excuse me for being in the way—tie them tight!"

"Yes, and his feet too, the villain!" cried the boys in great excitement, tying knot after knot with Herculean jerks.

The prisoner changed his tone.

"Oh-oh!" he moaned, "spare a poor sick man— I was but walking in my sleep."

"Ugh!" grunted Lambert, still tugging away at the rope, "asleep, were you? well, we'll wake you up."

The man muttered fierce oaths between his teeth —then cried in a piteous voice. "Unbind me, good young masters! I have five little children at home. By Saint Bavon I swear to give you each a ten-guilder piece if you will but free me!"

"Ha! ha!" laughed Peter.

"Ha! ha!" laughed the other boys.

Then came threats—threats that made Ludwig fairly shudder, though he continued to bind and tie with redoubled energy.

"Hold up! mynheer house-breaker," said Van Mounen in a warning voice. "That knife is very near your throat. If you make the captain nervous, there is no telling what may happen."

The robber took the hint, and fell into a sullen silence.

Just at this moment the chrysalis upon the bed stirred and sat erect.

"What's the matter?" he asked, without opening his eyes.

"Matter!" echoed Ludwig, half trembling, half laughing, "get up, Jacob. Here's work for you.

Come sit on this fellow's back while we get into our clothes, we're half perished."

"What fellow? Donder!"

"Hurrah for Poot!" cried all the boys, as Jacob sliding quickly to the floor, bed clothes and all, took in the state of affairs at a glance, and sat heavily beside Peter on the robber's back.

Oh, didn't the fellow groan, then!

"No use in holding him down any longer, boys," said Peter, rising, but bending as he did so to draw a pistol from his man's belt. "You see I've been keeping guard over this pretty little weapon for the last ten minutes. It's cocked and the least wriggle might have set it off. No danger now. I must dress myself. You and I, Lambert, will go for the police. I'd no idea it was so cold."

"Where is Carl?" asked one of the boys.

They looked at one another. Carl certainly was not among them.

"Oh!" cried Ludwig, frightened at last, "where is he? Perhaps he's had a fight with the robber, and got killed."

"Not a bit of it," said Peter quietly, as he buttoned his stout jacket. "Look under the beds."

They did so. Carl was not there.

Just then they heard a commotion on the stairway. Ben hastened to open the door. The landlord almost tumbled in; he was armed with a big blunderbuss. Two or three lodgers followed; then the daughter, with an up-raised frying-pan in one hand, and a candle in the other; and behind her, looking pale and frightened, the gallant Carl!

"There's your man, mine host," said Peter nodding toward the prisoner.

Mine host raised his blunderbuss, the girl screamed, and Jacob, more nimble than usual, rolled quickly from the robber's back.

"Don't fire," cried Peter, "he is tied, hand and foot. Let's roll him over, and see what he looks like."

Carl stepped briskly forward, with a blustering "Yes. We'll turn him over in a way he won't like. Lucky we've caught him!"

"Ha! ha!" laughed Ludwig, "where were you, Master Carl?"

"Where was I?" retorted Carl, angrily, "why, I went to give the alarm, to be sure!"

All the boys exchanged glances; but they were too happy and elated to say anything ill-natured. Carl certainly was bold enough now. He took the lead while three others aided him in turning the helpless man.

While the robber lay, face up, scowling and muttering, Ludwig took the candlestick from the girl's hand.

"I must have a good look at the beauty," he said drawing closer, but the words were no sooner spoken than he turned pale and started so violently that he almost dropped the candle.

"THE VOETSPOELEN!" he cried, "why, boys, it's the man who sat by the fire!"

"Of course it is," answered Peter, "we counted our money before him like simpletons. But what have we to do with voetspoelen, brother Ludwig? A month in jail is punishment enough."

The landlord's daughter had left the room She now ran in, holding up a pair of huge wooden shoes. "See, father," she cried, "here are his great ugly boots. It's the man that we put in the next room after the young masters went to bed. Ah! it was wrong to send the poor young gentlemen up here so far out of sight and sound."

"The scoundrel!" hissed the landlord, "he has disgraced my house. I go for the police at once!"

In less than fifteen minutes two drowsy looking officers were in the room. After telling Mynheer Kleef that he must appear early in the morning with the boys and make his complaint before a magistrate, they marched off with their prisoner.

CHAPTER XX

BEFORE THE COURT

You may believe the landlord's daughter bestirred herself to prepare a good meal for the boys next morning. Mynheer had a Chinese gong that could make more noise than a dozen of breakfast bells. Its hideous reveille, clanging through the house generally startled the drowsiest lodgers into activity, but the maiden would not allow it to be sounded this morning.

"Let the brave young gentlemen sleep," she said to the greasy kitchen-boy, "they shall be warmly fed when they awaken."

It was ten o'clock when Captain Peter and his band came straggling down one by one.

"A pretty hour," said mine host, gruffly. "It is high time we were before the court. Fine business this for a respectable inn. You will testify truly, young masters, that you found most excellent fare and lodgment at the Red Lion?"

"Of course we will," answered Carl, saucily, "and pleasant company, too, though they visit at rather unseasonable hours."

A stare and a "humph!" was all the answer Mynheer made to this, but the daughter was more communicative. Shaking her ear-rings at Carl she said sharply:

"Not so very pleasant either, master traveler, if one could judge by the way you ran away from it!"

"Impertinent creature!" hissed Carl under his breath, as he began busily to examine his skate-straps. Meantime the kitchen-boy, listening outside at the crack of the door, doubled himself with silent laughter.

After breakfast the boys went to the Police Court, accompanied by Huygens Kleef and his daughter. Mynheer's testimony was principally to the effect that such a thing as a robber at the "Red Lion" had been unheard of until last night; and as for the "Red Lion," it was a most respectable inn, as respectable as any house in Leyden. Each boy, in turn, told all he knew of the affair, and identified the prisoner in the box as the same man who entered their room in the dead of night. Ludwig was surprised to find that the robber was a man of ordinary size—especially after he had described him, under oath, to the Court as a tremendous fellow, with great square shoulders, and legs of prodigious weight. Jacob swore that he was awakened by the robber kicking and thrashing upon the floor; and, immediately afterward, Peter and the rest (feeling sorry that they had not explained the matter to their sleepy comrade) testified that the man had not moved a muscle from the moment the point of the dagger touched his throat, until, bound from head to foot, he was rolled over for inspection. The landlord's daughter made one boy blush, and all the court smile, by declaring that, "if it hadn't been for that handsome young gentleman there" (pointing to Peter) they "might have all been murdered in their beds; for the dreadful man had a great, shining knife most as long as your honor's arm," and she believed "the handsome young gentleman had struggled hard enough to get it away from him, but he was too modest, bless him! to say so."

Finally, after a little questioning, and cross-questioning from the public Prosecutor the witnesses were dismissed, and the robber was handed over to the consideration of the Criminal Court.

"The scoundrel!" said Carl, savagely, when the

boys reached the street. "He ought to be sent to jail at once. If I had been in your place, Peter, I certainly should have killed him outright!"

"He was fortunate, then, in falling into gentler hands," was Peter's quiet reply; "it appears he has been arrested before under a charge of house-breaking. He did not succeed in robbing this time, but he broke the door-fastenings, and that I believe makes a burglary in the eye of the law. He was armed with a knife, too, and that makes it worse for him, poor fellow!"

"Poor fellow!" mimicked Carl, "one would think he was your brother!"

"So he is my brother, and yours, too, Carl Schummel, for that matter," answered Peter, looking into Carl's eye. "We cannot say what we might have become under other circumstances. We have been bolstered up from evil, since the hour we were born. A happy home and good parents might have made that man a fine fellow instead of what he is. God grant that the law may cure and not crush him!"

"Amen to that!" said Lambert, heartily, while Ludwig van Holp looked at his brother in such a bright, proud way that Jacob Poot, who was an only son, wished from his heart that the little form buried in the old church at home had lived to grow up beside him.

"Humph!" said Carl, "It's very well to be saintly and forgiving, and all that sort of thing, but I'm naturally hard. All these fine ideas seem to rattle off of me like hail-stones—and it's nobody's business either, if they do."

Peter recognized a touch of good feeling in this clumsy concession; holding out his hand, he said in a frank, hearty tone:

"Come, lad, shake hands, and let us be good friends, even if we don't exactly agree on all questions."

"We do agree better than you think," sulked Carl, as he returned Peter's grasp.

"All right," responded Peter briskly, "now, Van Mounen, we await Benjamin's wishes. Where would he like to go?"

"To the Egyptian Museum," answered Lambert, after holding a brief consultation with Ben.

"That is on the Breede Straat. To the Museum let it be. Come, boys!"

CHAPTER XXI

THE BELEAGUERED CITIES

"This open square before us," said Lambert, as he and Ben walked on together, "is pretty in Summer, with its shady trees. They call it the Ruine. Years ago it was covered with houses, and the Rapenburg canal, here, ran through the street. Well, one day a barge loaded with forty thousand pounds of gunpowder, bound for Delft, was lying alongside, and the bargemen took a notion to cook their dinner on the deck; and before anyone knew it, sir, the whole thing blew up, killing lots of persons and scattering about three hundred houses to the winds."

"What!" exclaimed Ben, "did the explosion destroy three hundred houses?"

"Yes, sir, my father was in Leyden at the time. He says it was terrible. The explosion occurred just at noon, and was like a volcano. All this part of the town was on fire in an instant, buildings tumbling down, and men, women and children groaning under the ruins—The King himself came to the city and acted nobly, father says, staying out in the streets all night, encouraging the survivors in their efforts to arrest the fire, and rescue as many as possible from under the heaps of stone and rubbish. Through his means a collection for the benefit of the sufferers was raised throughout the kingdom, besides a hundred thousand guilders paid out of the treasury. Father was only nineteen years old then; it was in 1807 I believe, but he remembers it perfectly. A friend of his, Professor Lusac, was among the killed. They have a tablet erected to his memory, in Saint Peter's Church, further on!—the queerest thing you ever saw—with an image of the pro-

fessor carved upon it representing him just as he
looked when he was found after the explosion."

"What a strange idea! Isn't Boerhaave's monument in Saint Peter's also?"

"I cannot remember. Perhaps Peter knows."

The captain delighted Ben by saying that the
monument was there and that he thought they might
be able to see it during the day.

"Lambert," continued Peter, "ask Ben if he saw
Van der Werf's portrait at the Town Hall last
night."

"No," said Lambert, "I can answer for him. It
was too late to go in. I say, boys, it is really wonderful how much Ben knows. Why, he has told me
a volume of Dutch history already. I'll wager he has
the siege of Leyden at his tongue's end."

"His tongue must burn then," interposed Ludwig,
"for if Bilderdyk's account is true it was a pretty
hot affair."

Ben was looking at them with an inquiring smile.

"We are speaking of the siege of Leyden," explained Lambert.

"Oh, yes," said Ben, eagerly, "I had forgotten all
about it. This was the very place—Let's give old
Van der Werf three cheers—Hur—"

Van Mounen uttered a hasty "hush!" and exclaimed that, patriotic as the Dutch were, the police
would soon have something to say if a party of boys
cheered in the street at mid-day.

"What! not cheer Van der Werf?" cried Ben, indignantly. "One of the greatest chaps in history?
Only think! Didn't he hold out against those mur-
derous Spaniards for months and months! There
was the town, surrounded on all sides by the enemy;
great black forts sending fire and death into the
very heart of the city—but no surrender! Every

man a hero—women, and children, too, brave and
fierce as lions—provisions giving out, the very grass
from between the paving stones gone—till people
were glad to eat horses and cats and dogs and rats.
Then came the Plague—hundreds dying in the
streets—but no surrender! Then when they could
bear no more—when the people, brave as they were,
crowded about Van der Werf in the public square
begging him to give up; what did the noble old
burgomaster say:—'I have sworn to defend this city,
and with God's help I mean to do it. If my body
can satisfy your hunger, take it, and divide it among
you—but expect no surrender as long as I am alive'
—Hurrah! hur—"

Ben was getting uproarious; Lambert playfully
clapped his hand over his friend's mouth. The
result was one of those quick india-rubber scuffles
fearful to behold, but delightful to human nature in
its polliwog state.

"Vat wash te matter, Ben?" asked Jacob, hurrying
forward.

"Oh! nothing at all," panted Ben, "except that
Van Mounen was afraid of starting an English riot
in this orderly town. He stopped my cheering for
old Van der—"

"Ya! ya—it ish no good to sheer—to make te
noise for dat—You vill shee old Van der Does' likeness mit to Stadhuis."

"See old Van der Does? I thought it was Van
der Werf's picture they had there—"

"Ya." responded Jacob, "Van der Werf—vell, vot
of it! both ish just ash goot—"

"Yes, Van der Does was a noble old Dutchman,
but he was not Van der Werf. I know he defended
the city like a brick, and—"

"Now vot for you shay dat, Penchamin? He no

defend te city mit breek, he fight like goot soltyer mit his guns. You like make te fun mit effrysinks Tutch."

"No! no! no! I said he defended the city like a brick. That is very high praise, I would have you understand. We English call even the Duke of Wellington a brick."

Jacob looked puzzled; but his indignation was already on the ebb:

"Vell it ish no matter. I no tink, before, soltyer mean breek, but it ish no matter."

Ben laughed good-naturedly, and seeing that his cousin was tired of talking in English, he turned to his friend of the two languages—

"Van Mounen! they say the very carrier-pigeons that brought news of relief to the besieged city, are somewhere here in Leyden. I really should like to see them. Just think of it! At the very height of the trouble if the wind didn't turn, and blow in the waters, and drown hundreds of the Spaniards, and enable the Dutch boats to sail in right over the land with men and provisions to the very gates of the city. The pigeons, you know, did great service, in bearing letters to and fro. I have read, somewhere that they were reverently cared for from that day, and, when they died, they were stuffed, and placed for safe keeping in the Town Hall. We must be sure to have a look at them."

Van Mounen laughed. "On that principal, Ben, I suppose when you go to Rome you'll expect to see the identical goose who saved the Capitol. But it will be easy enough to see the pigeons. They are in the same building with Van der Werf's portrait. Which was the greatest defense, Ben, the siege of Leyden or the siege of Haarlem?"

"Well," replied Ben, thoughtfully; "Van der Werf

is one of my heroes; we all have our historical pets,
you know, but I really think the siege of Haarlem
brought out a braver, more heroic resistance even,
than the Leyden one; besides they set the Leyden
sufferers an example of courage and fortitude, for
their turn came first."

"I don't know much about the Haarlem siege,"
said Lambert, "except that it was in 1573. Who
beat?"

"The Spaniards," said Ben. "The Dutch had stood
out for months. Not a man would yield nor a woman either for that matter. They shouldered arms
and fought gallantly beside their husbands and
fathers. Three hundred of them did duty under
Kanau Hesselaer, a great woman, and brave as
Joan of Arc. All this time the city was surrounded
by the Spaniards under Frederic of Toledo, son of
that beauty, the Duke of Alva. Cut off from all
possible help from without, there seemed to be no
hope for the inhabitants, but they shouted defiance
over the city walls. They even threw bread into the
enemy's camps to show that they were not afraid of
starvation. Up to the last they held out bravely,
waiting for the help that never could come—growing bolder and bolder until their provisions were
exhausted. Then it was terrible. In time hundreds
of famished creatures fell dead in the streets, and
the living had scarcely strength to bury them. At
last, they made the desperate resolution, that rather
than perish by lingering torture, the strongest would
form in a square, placing the weakest in the center,
and rush in a body to their death, with the faint
chance of being able to fight their way through the
enemy. The Spaniards received a hint of this, and
believing there was nothing the Dutch would not
dare to do, they concluded to offer terms.

"High time I should think."

"Yes, with falsehood and treachery they soon obtained an entrance into the city, promising protection and forgiveness to all except those whom the citizens themselves would acknowledge as deserving of death."

"You don't say so!" said Lambert, quite interested, "that ended the business I suppose."

"Not a bit of it," returned Ben, "for the Duke of Alva had already given his son orders to show mercy to none."

"Ah, there was where the great Haarlem massacre came in. I remember now. You can't wonder that the Hollanders dislike Spain when you read of the way they were butchered by Alva and his hosts, though I admit that our side sometimes retaliated terribly. But as I have told you before, I have a very indistinct idea of historical matters. Everything is utter confusion—from the Flood to the battle of Waterloo. One thing is plain, however, the Duke of Alva was about the worst specimen of a man that ever lived."

"That gives only a faint idea of him," said Ben, "but I hate to think of such a wretch. What if he had brains, and military skill, and all that sort of thing! Give me such men as Van der Werf, and—what now?"

"Why," said Van Mounen, who was looking up and down the street, in a bewildered way. "We've walked right past the museum, and I don't see the boys. Let us go back."

CHAPTER XXII

The boys met at the Museum, and were soon engaged in examining its extensive collection of curiosities, receiving a new insight into Egyptian life, ancient and modern. Ben and Lambert had often visited the British Museum, but that did not prevent them from being surprised at the richness of the Leyden collection. There were household utensils, wearing apparel, weapons, musical instruments, sarcophagi, and mummies of men, women, and cats, ibexes and other creatures. They saw a massive gold armlet that had been worn by an Egyptian King at a time when some of these same mummies, perhaps, were nimbly treading the streets of Thebes; and jewels and trinkets such as Pharaoh's daughter wore, and the children of Israel borrowed when they departed out of Egypt.

There were other interesting relics, from Rome and Greece, and some curious Roman pottery, which had been discovered in digging near the Hague—relics of the days when the countrymen of Julius Caesar had settled there. Where have they not settled? I for one, would hardly be astonished if relics of the ancient Romans should some day be found deep under the grass growing round the Bunkerhill monument.

When the boys left this Museum, they went to another, and saw a wonderful collection of fossil animals, skeletons, birds, minerals, precious stones and other natural specimens, but as they were not learned men, they could only walk about and stare, enjoy the little knowledge of natural history they possessed, and wish with all their hearts they had ac-

quired more. Even the skeleton of the mouse puzzled Jacob. What wonder? He was not used to
seeing the cat-fearing little creatures running about
in their bones—and how could he ever have imag-
ined their necks to be so queer?

Besides the Museum of Natural History, there
was Saint Peter's Church to be visited, containing
Professor Luzac's Memorial, and Boerhaave's Monument of white and black marble, with its urn and
carved symbols of the four ages of life, and its me-
dallion of Boerhaave, adorned with his favorite motto "simplex sigillum veri." They also obtained ad-
mittance to a tea-garden, which in summer was a
favorite resort of the citizens, and passing naked
oaks and fruit-trees, ascended a high mound which
stood in the center. This was the site of a round
tower now in ruins, said by some to have been built
by Hengist the Anglo-Saxon king, and by others to
have been the castle of one of the ancient counts of
Holland.

As the boys walked about on the top of its stone
wall, they could get but a poor view of the surrounding city. The tower stood higher when, more than
two centuries ago, the inhabitants of beleagured
Leyden shouted to the watcher on its top, their wild,
despairing cries—"Is there any help? Are the
waters rising? What do you see?"

And for months he could only answer—"No help.
I see around us nothing but the enemy."

Ben pushed these thoughts away; and resolutely
looking down into the bare tea-garden, filled it in
imagination with gay Summer groups. He tried to
forget old battle-clouds, and picture only curling
wreaths of tobacco-smoke, rising from among men,
women and children enjoying their tea and coffee in
the open air. But a tragedy came in spite of him.

Poot was bending over the edge of the high wall.
It would be just like him to grow dizzy and tumble
off. Ben turned impatiently away. If the fellow
with his weak head knew no better than to be venturesome, why, let him tumble. Horror! what meant
that heavy, crashing sound?

Ben could not stir. He could only gasp.

"Jacob!"

"Jacob!" cried another startled voice and another.
Ready to faint, Ben managed to turn his head. He
saw a crowd of boys on the edge of the wall opposite
—but Jacob was not there!

"Good Heaven!" he cried, springing forward,
"where is my cousin?"

The crowd parted. It was only four boys, after
all. There sat Jacob in their midst, holding his sides
and laughing heartily.

"Did I frighten you all?" he said in his native
Dutch, "well I will tell you how it was. There was
a big stone lying on the wall and I put my—my foot
out just to push it a little, you see—and the first
thing I knew, down went the stone all the way to the
bottom, and left me sitting here on top with both my
feet in the air. If I had not thrown myself back
at that moment, I certainly should have rolled over
after the stone. Well, it is no matter. Help me up,
boys."

"You are hurt, Jacob!" cried Ben, seeing a shade
of seriousness pass over his cousin's face as they
lifted him to his feet.

Jacob tried to laugh again. "Oh, no—I feels little
hurt vent I stand up, but it ish no matter."

The monument to Van der Werf in the Hoogland-
sche Kerk was not accessible that day; but the boys
spent a few pleasant moments in the Stadhuis or
Town Hall, a long irregular structure somewhat in

the Gothic style, uncouth in architecture, but picturesque from age. Its little steeple, tuneful with
bells, seemed to have been borrowed from some other
building and hastily clapped on as a finishing touch.

Ascending the grand staircase the boys soon found
themselves in rather a gloomy apartment, containing the master piece of Lucas van Leyden, or Hu-
gens, a Dutch artist, born three hundred and seven-
ty years ago, who painted well when he was ten
years of age and became distinguished in art when
only fifteen. This picture, called the Last Judgment,
considering the remote age in which it was painted,
is truly a remarkable production. The boys, however, were less interested in tracing out the merits
of the work than they were in the fact of its being
a triptych—that is painted on three divisions, the
two outer ones swung on hinges so as to close, when
required, over the main portion.

The historical pictures by Harel de Moor and
other famous Dutch artists interested them for
awhile, and Ben had to be almost pulled away from
the dingy old portrait of Van der Werf.

Ben, as he scanned the buildings on the Rapenburg canal, was somewhat disappointed in the appearance of the great University of Leyden. But
when he recalled its history—how, attended with all
the pomp of a grand civic display, it had been found-
ed by the Prince of Orange, as a tribute to the citizens for the bravery displayed during the siege;
when he remembered the great men in religion,
learning and science who had once studied there, and
thought of the hundreds of students now sharing the
benefits of its classes and its valuable scientific mu-
seums—he was quite willing to forego architectural
beauty, though he could not help feeling that no

amount of it could have been misplaced on such an institution.

Peter and Jacob regarded the building with even a deeper, more practical interest, for they were to enter it as students, in the course of a few months.

"Poor Don Quixote would have run a hopeless tilt in this part of the world," said Ben, after Lambert had been pointing out some of the oddities and beauties of the suburbs—"it is all windmills. You remember his terrific contest with one, I suppose."

"No," said Lambert, bluntly.

"Well, I don't either, that is, not definitely. But there was something of that kind in his adventures, and if there wasn't there should have been—Look at them, how frantically they whirl their great arms —just the thing to excite the crazy knight to mortal combat. It bewilders one to look at them; help me to count all those we can see, Van Mounen. I want a big item for my notebook"—and after a careful reckoning, superintended by all the party, Master Ben wrote in pencil, "Saw, Dec.—, 184—, ninety-eight windmills within full view of Leyden."

He would have been glad to visit the old brick mill in which the painter Rembrandt was born; but he abandoned the project upon learnng that it would take them out of their way. Few boys as hungry as Ben was by this time would hesitate long between Rembrandt's home a mile off and tiffin close by. Ben chose the latter.

After tiffin, they rested awhile, and then—took another, which, for form's sake, they called dinner. After dinner the boys sat warming themselves, at the inn; all but Peter, who occupied the time in another fruitless search for Dr. Boekman.

This over, the party once more prepared for skating. They were thirteen miles from the Hague and not as fresh as when they left Broek early on the previous day, but they were in good spirits and the ice was excellent.

CHAPTER XXIII

THE PALACE AND THE MOON

As the boys skated onward, they saw a number of fine country seats, all decorated and surrounded according to the Dutchest of Dutch taste, but impressive to look upon, with their great, formal houses, elaborate gardens, square hedges and wide ditches —everywhere traversing the landscape, had long ago lost their summer film, and now shone under the sunlight, like trailing ribbons of glass.

The boys traveled bravely, all the while performing the surprising feat of producing gingerbread from their pockets and causing it to vanish instantly.

Twelve miles were passed. A few more long strokes would take them to the Hague, when Van Mounen proposed that they should vary their course, by walking into the city through The Bosch.

"Agreed!" cried one and all—and their skates were off in a twinkling.

The Bosch is a grand park or wood, nearly two miles long, containing the celebrated House in the Wood—*Huis in't Bosch*—sometimes used as a royal residence.

This building, though plain outside for a palace, is elegantly furnished within, and finely frescoed— that is, the walls and ceilings are covered with groups and designs painted directly upon them while the plaster was fresh. Some of the rooms are tapestried with Chinese silk, beautifully embroidered. One contains a number of family portraits, among them a group of royal children who in time were orphaned by a certain axe which figures very frequently in European history. These children were painted many times by the Dutch artist Van Dyck,

who was court painter to their father, Charles the
First of England. Beautiful children they were—
what a deal of trouble the English nation would have
been spared, had they been as perfect in heart and
soul, as they were in form!

The park surrounding the palace is charming,
especially in summer, for flowers and birds make it
bright as fairyland. Long rows of magnificent oaks
rear their proud heads, conscious that no profaning
hand will ever bring them low. In fact the Wood
has for ages been held as an almost sacred spot.
Children are never allowed to meddle with its smallest twig; the axe of the Woodman has never re-
sounded there. Even war and riot have passed it
reverently, pausing for a moment in their devas-
tating way. Philip of Spain, while he ordered
Dutchmen to be mowed down by hundreds, issued
a mandate that not a bough of the beautiful Wood
should be touched—and once when in a time of great
necessity the State was about to sacrifice it to assist
in filling a nearly exhausted treasury, the people
rushed to the rescue, and nobly contributed the required amount rather than that the Bosch should
fall.

What wonder then that the oaks have a grand,
fearless air? Birds from all Holland have told them
how, elsewhere, trees are cropped and bobbed into
shape—but they are untouched. Year after year,
they expand in unclipped luxuriance and beauty;
their wide-spreading foliage, alive with song, casts a
cool shade over lawn and path-way, or bows to its
image in the sunny ponds.

Meanwhile, as if to reward the citizens for allowing her to have her way for once, Nature departs
from the invariable level, wearing gracefully the
ornaments that have been reverently bestowed upon

her—so the lawn slopes in a velvety green; the paths
wind in and out; flower-beds glow and send forth
perfume; and ponds and sky look at each other in
mutual admiration.

Even on that winter day the Bosch was beautiful.
Its trees were bare, but beneath them still lay the
ponds, every ripple smoothed into glass. The blue
sky was bright overhead, and as it looked down
through the thicket of boughs, it saw another blue
sky, not nearly so bright, looking up from the dim
thicket under the ice.

Never had the sunset appeared more beautiful to
Peter than when he saw it exchanging farewell
glances with the windows and shining roofs of the
city before him. Never had the Hague itself seemed
more inviting. He was no longer Peter van Holp,
going to visit a great city, nor a fine young gentleman bent on sight-seeing; he was a night, an adven-
turer, travel-soiled and weary, a Hop-o'-my-Thumb
grown large, a Fortunatus approaching the enchanted castle where luxury and ease awaited him—for
his own sister's house was not half a mile away.

"At last, boys," he cried, in high glee, "we may
hope for a royal resting-place—good beds, warm
rooms, and something fit to eat. I never realized
before what a luxury such things are. Our lodgings
at the Red Lion have made us appreciate our own
homes."

CHAPTER XXIV

THE MERCHANT PRINCE, AND THE SISTER-PRINCESS

Well might Peter feel that his sister's house was like an enchanted castle. Large and elegant as it was, a spell of quiet hung over it. The very lion crouching at its gate seemed to have been turned into stone through magic. Within, it was guarded by genii, in the shape of red-faced servants, who sprang silently forth at the summons of bell or knocker. There was a cat, also, who appeared as knowing as any Puss-in-Boots; and a brass gnome in the hall whose business it was to stand with outstretched arms ready to receive sticks and umbrellas. Safe within the walls bloomed a Garden of Delight, where flowers firmly believed it was summer, and a sparkling fountain was laughing merrily to itself because Jack Frost could not find it. There was a Sleeping Beauty, too, just at the time of the boys' arrival; but when Peter, like a true prince, flew lightly up the stairs, and kissed her eyelids, the enchantment was broken. The princess became his own good sister, and the fairy castle just one of the finest, most comfortable houses of the Hague.

As may well be believed, the boys received the heartiest of welcomes. After they had conversed awhile with their lively hostess, one of the genii summoned them to a grand repast in a red-curtained room, where floor and ceiling shone polished ivory, and the mirrors suddenly blossomed into rosy-cheeked boys as far as the eye could reach.

They had caviare now, and salmagundi, and sausage and cheese, besides salad and fruit and biscuit and cake. How the boys could partake of such a medley was a mystery to Ben; for the salad was sour, and the cake was sweet; the fruit was dainty, and the salmagundi heavy with onions and fish. But, while he was wondering, he made a hearty meal, and was soon absorbed in deciding which he really preferred, the coffee or the anisette cordial. It was delightful, too—this taking one's food from dishes of frosted silver and liqueur glasses from which Titania herself might have sipped. The young gentleman afterward wrote to his mother that pretty and choice as things were at home, he had never known what cut glass, china and silver services were until he visited the Hague.

Of course Peter's sister soon heard of all the boys' adventures. How they had skated over forty miles and seen rare sights on the way; how they had lost their purse and found it again. How one of the party had fallen and given them an excuse for a grand sail in an ice-boat; how above all, they had caught a robber, and so for a second time saved their slippery purse.

"And now, Peter," said the lady, when the story was finished, "you must write at once to tell the good people of Broek that your adventures have reached their height, that you and your fellow-travelers have all been taken prisoners."

The boys looked startled.

"Indeed, I shall do no such thing," laughed Peter, "we must leave to-morrow at noon."

But the sister had already decided differently, and a Holland lady is not to be easily turned from her purpose. In short, she held forth such strong temptations, and was so bright and cheerful, and said so many coaxing and unanswerable things, both in English and Dutch, that the boys were all delighted when it was settled that they should remain at the Hague for at least two days.

Next the grand skating-race was talked over;
Mevrouw van Gend gladly promised to be present on
the occasion—"I shall witness your triumph, Peter,"
she said, "for you are the fastest skater I ever
knew."

Peter blushed and gave a slight cough, as Carl
answered for him.

"Ah, mevrouw, he is swift, but all the Broek boys
are fine skaters—even the rag-pickers"—and he
thought bitterly of poor Hans.

The lady laughed. "That will make the race all
the more exciting," she said—"but I shall wish each
of you to be the winner."

At this moment her husband Mynheer van Gend
came in, and the enchantment falling upon the boys
was complete.

The invisible fairies of the household at once clustered about them whispering that Jasper van Gend
had a heart as young and fresh as their own, and if
he loved anything in this world, more than industry,
it was sunshine and frolic. They hinted also something about his having a heart full of love and head
full of wisdom, and finally gave the boys to understand that when Mynheer said a thing he meant it.

Therefore his frank "well now, this is pleasant,"
as he shook hands with them all, made the boys feel
quite at home and as happy as squirrels.

There were fine paintings in the drawing-room
and exquisite statuary, and portfolios filled with rare
Dutch engravings; besides many beautiful and curious things from China and Japan. The boys felt
that it would require a month to examine all the treasures of the apartment.

Ben noticed with pleasure English books lying upon the table. He saw also over the carved upright
piano, life-sized portraits of William of Orange and

his English queen, a sight that, for a time brought
England and Holland side by side in his heart. William and Mary have left a halo round the English
throne to this day, he the truest patriot that ever
served an adopted country, she the noblest wife
that ever sat upon a British throne, up to the time
of Victoria and Albert the Good. As Ben looked
at the pictures, he remembered accounts he had read
of King William's visit to the Hague in the winter
of 1691. He who sang the Battle of Ivry had not yet
told the glowing story of that day, but Ben knew
enough of it to fancy that he could almost hear the
shouts of the delighted populace as he looked from
the portraits to the street, which at this moment
was aglow with a bon-fire, kindled in a neighboring
square.

That royal visit was one never to be forgotten.
For two years William of Orange had been monarch
of a foreign land, his head working faithfully for
England, but his whole heart yearning for Holland.
Now when he sought its shores once more, the entire
nation bade him welcome. Multitudes flocked to the
Hague to meet him—"many thousands came sliding
or skating along the frozen canals from Amsterdam,
Rotterdam, Leyden, Haarlem, Delft." All day long
the festivities of the capital were kept up, the
streets were gorgeous with banners, evergreen
arches, trophies, and mottoes of welcome and em-
blems of industry. William saw the deeds of his
ancestors and scenes of his own past life, depicted
on banners and tapestries along the streets. At
night, superb fireworks were displayed upon the ice.
Its glassy surface was like a mirror. Sparkling
fountains of light sprang up from below to meet the
glittering cascades leaping upon it. Then a feathery
fire of crimson and green shook millions of rubies

and emeralds into the ruddy depths of the ice—and all this time the people were shouting—God bless William of Orange—long live the King! They were half mad with joy and enthusiasm. William their own prince, their stadt-holder, had become the ruler of three kingdoms; he had been victorious in council and in war, and now in his hour of greatest triumph, had come as a simple guest to visit them. The king heard their shouts with a beating heart. It is a great thing to be beloved by one's country. His English courtiers complimented him upon his reception. "Yes," said he, "but the shouting is nothing to what it would have been if Mary had been with me!"

While Ben was looking at the portraits, Mynheer van Gend was giving the boys an account of a recent visit to Antwerp. As it was the birthplace of Quentin Matsys, the blacksmith who for love of an artist's daughter, studied until he became a great painter, the boys asked their host if he had seen any of Matsys' works.

"Yes, indeed," he replied, "and excellent they are. His famous triptych in a chapel of the Antwerp cathedral with the Descent from the Cross on the center panel, is especially fine; but I confess I was more interested in his well."

"What well, mynheer?" asked Ludwig.

"One in the heart of the city, near this same Cathedral whose lofty steeple is of such delicate workmanship, that the French Emperor said it reminded him of Mechlin lace. The well is covered with a gothic canopy surmounted by the figure of a knight in full armor. It is all of metal, and proves that Matsys was an artist at the forge as well as at the easel; indeed his great fame is mainly derived from his miraculous skill as an artificer in iron."

Next, mynheer showed the boys some exquisite
Berlin castings, which he had purchased in Antwerp.
They were iron jewelry, and very delicate—beautiful medallions designed from rare paintings, bordered with fine tracery and open work—worthy he said
of being worn by the fairest lady of the land. Consequently the necklace was handed with a bow and a
smile to the blushing Mevrouw van Gend.

Something in the lady's aspect, as she bent her
bright young face over the gift, caused mynheer to
add earnestly.

"I can read your thoughts, sweetheart."

She looked up in playful defiance.

"Ah! now I am sure of them. You were thinking
of those noble-hearted women, but for whom Prussia
might have fallen. I know it by that proud light
in your eye."

"The proud light in my eye plays me false, then,"
she answered, "I had no such grand matter in my
mind. To confess the simple truth, I was thinking
how lovely this necklace would be with my blue bro-
cade."

"So! so!" exclaimed the rather crest-fallen spouse.

"But I can think of the other, Jasper, and it will
add a deeper value to your gift. You remember the
incident do you not, Peter? How, when the French
were invading Prussia and for lack of means, the
country was unable to defend itself against the
enemy, the women turned the scale by pouring their
plate and jewels into the public treasury—"

"Aha!" thought mynheer, as he met his vrouw's
kindling glance. "The proud light is there, now, in
earnest."

Peter remarked maliciously that the women had
still proved true to their vanity on that occasion, for
jewelry they would have. If gold or silver were

wanted by the kingdom, they would relinquish it
and use iron, but they could not do without their
ornaments.

"What of that?" said the vrouw, kindling again.
"It is no sin to love beautiful things, if you adapt
your material to circumstances. All I have to say is,
the women saved their country and, indirectly, intro-
duced a very important branch of manufacture. Is
not that so, Jasper?"

"Of course it is, sweetheart," said mynheer, "but
Peter needs no word of mine to convince him that
all the world over, women have never been found
wanting in their country's hour of trial, though
(bowing to Mevrouw) his own countrywomen stand
foremost in the records of female patriotism and de-
votion."

Then turning to Ben, the host talked with him in
English of the fine old Belgian city. Among other
things, he told the origin of its name. Ben had been
taught that Atnwerp was derived from ae'nt werf
(on the wharf), but Mynheer van Gend gave him
a far more interesting derivation.

It appears that about three thousand years ago,
a great giant, named Antigonus, lived on the river
Scheld, on the site of the present city of Antwerp.
This giant claimed half the merchandise of all navi-
gators who passed his castle. Of course some were .
inclined to oppose this simple regulation. In such
cases, Antigonus, by way of teaching them to practice better manners next time, cut off and threw into
the river, the right hands of the merchants. Thus
hand-werpen (or hand-throwing), changed to Antwerp, came to be the name of the place. The escut-
cheon or arms of the city has two hands upon it;
what better proof than this could one have of the

truth of the story, especially when one wishes to believe it!

The giant was finally conquered and thrown into
the Scheld by a hero called Brabo, who in turn gave
a name to the district known as Brabant.   Since
then the Dutch merchants have traveled the river in
peace; but I for one, thank old Antigonus for giving
the city so romantic an origin.

When Mynheer van Gend had related in two languages this story of Antwerp, he was tempted to
tell other legends—some in English, some in Dutch;
and so the moments, borne upon the swift shoulders
of gnomes and giants, glided rapidly away toward
bed-time.

It was hard to break up so pleasant a party, but
the Van Gend household moved with the regularity
of clockwork.   There was no lingering at the threshold when the cordial "goodnight!" was spoken.
Even while our boys were mounting the stairs, the
invisible household fairies again clustered around
them, whispering that system and regularity had
been chief builders of the master's prosperity.

Beautiful chambers with three beds in them were
not to be found in this mansion.   Some of the rooms
contained two, but each visitor slept alone.   Before
morning, the motto of the party evidently was,
"every boy his own chrysalis"—and Peter, at least,
was not sorry to have it so.

Tired as he was, Ben after noting a curious bell-
rope in the corner, began to examine his bed-clothes.
Each article filled him with astonishment—the exquisite fine pillow-spread trimmed with costly lace
and embroidered with a gorgeous crest and initial,
the dekbed cover a great silk bag, large as the bed,
stuffed with swansdown and the pink satin quilts,

embroidered with garlands of flowers. He could scarcely sleep for thinking what a queer little bed it was, so comfortable and pretty, too, with all its queerness. In the morning he examined the top coverlet with care, for he wished to send home a description of it in his next letter. It was a Japanese spread, marvelous in texture as well as in its variety of brilliant coloring, and worth, as Ben afterward learned not less than three hundred dollars.

The floor was of polished wooden mosaic, nearly covered with a rich carpet bordered with thick, black fringe. Another room displayed a margin of satin-wood around the carpet. Hung with tapestry, its walls of crimson silk were topped with a gilded cornice which shot down gleams of light far into the polished floor.

Over the door-way of the room in which Jacob and Ben slept was a bronze stork who, with outstretched neck, held a lamp to light the guests into the apartment. Between the two narrow beds, of carved white-wood and ebony, stood the household treasure of the Van Gends, a massive oaken chair upon which the Prince of Orange had once sat, during a council meeting. Opposite, stood a quaintly carved clothes-press, waxed and polished to the utmost, and filled with precious stores of linen; beside it a table holding a large Bible, whose great golden clasps looked poor compared with its solid, ribbed binding made to outlast six generations.

There was a ship model on the mantel-shelf, and over it hung an old portrait of Peter the Great, who, you know, once gave the dock-yard cats of Holland a fine chance to look at a king, which is one of the special prerogatives of cats. Peter, though czar of Russia, was not too proud to work as a common ship-

wright in the dockyards of Saardam and Amsterdam, that he might be able to introduce among his
countrymen Dutch improvements in ship-building.
It was this willingness to be thorough in even the
smallest beginnings that earned for him the title of
Peter the Great.

Peter the little (comparatively speaking) was up
first, the next morning; knowing the punctual habits
of his brother-in-law, he took good care that none
of the boys should oversleep themselves. A hard
task he found it to wake Jacob Poot; but after pulling that young gentleman out of bed, and, with
Ben's help dragging him about the room for awhile,
he succeeded in arousing him.

While Jacob was dressing, and moaning within
him, because the felt slippers, provided him as a
guest, were too tight for his swollen feet, Peter
wrote to inform their friends at Broek of the safe
arrival of his party at the Hague. He also begged
his mother to send word to Hans Brinker that Dr.
Boekman had not yet reached Leyden, but that a
letter containing Hans' message had been left at
the Hotel, where the doctor always lodged during his
visits to the city. "Tell him, also," wrote Peter,
"that I shall call there again, as I pass through Leyden. The poor boy seemed to feel sure that 'the
meester' would hasten to save his father, but we,
who know the gruff old gentleman better, may be
confident he will do no such thing. It would be a
kindness to send a visiting physician from Amsterdam to the cottage at once, if Jufvrouw* Brinker
will consent to receive any but the great king of the
meesters as Dr. Boekman certainly is.

*In Holland, women of the lower grades of society do not
take the title of Mrs. (or Mevrouw) when they marry, as with
us. They assume their husband's name, but are still called
Miss (Jufvrouw, pronounced Juffrow).

"You know, mother," added Peter, "that I have always considered Sister van Gend's house as rather quiet and lonely; but I assure you, it is not so now. Sister says our presence has warmed it for the whole winter. Brother van Gend is very kind to us all. He says we make him wish he had a houseful of boys of his own. He has promised to let us ride on his noble black horses. They are gentle as kittens, he says, if one have but a firm touch at the rein. Ben, according to Jacob's account, is a glorious rider, and your son Peter is not a very bad hand at the business; so we two are to go out together this morning mounted like knights of old. After we return, Brother van Gend says he will lend Jacob his English pony and obtain three extra horses; and all of the party are to trot about the city, in a grand cavalcade, led on by him. He will ride the black horse which father sent him from Friesland. My sister's pretty roan with the long white tail, is lame and she will ride none other; else she would accompany us. I could scarce close my eyes last night after sister told me of the plan. Only the thought of poor Hans Brinker and his sick father checked me—but for that I could have sung for joy. Ludwig has given us a name already—the Broek Cavalry. We flatter ourselves that we shall make an imposing appearance, especially in single file   .   .   .   ."

The Broek Cavalry were not disappointed. Mynheer van Gend readily procured good horses; and all the boys could ride, though none were as perfect horsemen or horseboys as Peter and Ben. They saw the Hague to their hearts' content; and the Hague saw them—expressing its approbation, loudly, through the mouths of small boys and cart-dogs; silently, through bright eyes that, not looking very deeply into things, shone as they looked at the handsome Carl, and twinkled with fun as a certain portly youth with shaking cheeks rode past "bumpety, bumpety, bump!"

On their return, the boys pronounced the great porcelain stove in the family sitting room a decidedly useful piece of furniture, for they could gather round it and get warm without burning their noses or bringing on chilblains. It was so very large that it seemed to send out warmth by the houseful—its pure white sides and polished brass rings, made it a pretty object to look upon, notwithstanding the fact that our ungrateful Ben, while growing thoroughly warm and comfortable beside it, concocted a satirical sentence for his next letter, to the effect that a stove in Holland must of course resemble a great tower of snow or it wouldn't be in keeping with the oddity of the country.

To describe all the boys saw and did on that day and the next, would render this little book a formidable volume indeed. They visited the brass cannon foundry, saw the liquid fire poured into moulds and watched the smiths who, half naked, stood in the shadow, like demons playing with flame. They admired the grand public buildings and massive private houses, the elegant streets, and noble Bosch —pride of all beauty-loving Hollanders. The palace with its brilliant mosaic floors, its frescoed ceilings and gorgeous ornaments, filled Ben with delight; he was surprised that some of the churches were so very plain—elaborate sometimes in external architecture, but bare and bleak within their blank, whitewashed walls.

If there were no printed record, the churches of Holland would almost tell her story. I will not enter into the subject here. except to say that Ben—who had read of her struggles and wrongs, and of the

terrible retribution she from time to time dealt forth
—could scarcely tread a Holland town without men-
tally leaping horror-stricken over the bloody step-
ping-stones of its history. He could not forget
Philip of Spain nor the duke of Alva even while
rejoicing in the prosperity that followed the Libera-
tion. He looked in the meekest of Dutch eyes, for
something of the fire that once lit the haggard faces
of those desperate, lawless men, who wearing with
pride the title of "Beggars" which their oppressors
had mockingly cast upon them, became the terror
of land and sea. In Haarlem, he had wondered that
the air did not still resound with the cries of Alva's
three thousand victims. In Leyden, his heart had
swelled in sympathy as he thought of the long pro-
cession of scarred and famished creatures who
after the siege, with Adrian van der Werf at their
head, tottered to the great church to sing a glorious
anthem because Leyden was free! He remembered
that this was even before they had tasted the bread
brought by the Dutch ships. They would praise
God first, then eat. Thousands of trembling voices
were raised in glad thanksgiving. For a moment, it
swelled higher and higher—then suddenly changed
to sobbing—not one of all the multitude could sing
another note. But who shall say that the anthem,
even to its very end, was not heard in Heaven!

Here, in the Hague, other thoughts came to Ben—
Of how Holland in later years unwillingly put her
head under the French yoke, and how, galled and
lashed past endurance, she had resolutely jerked it
out again. He liked her for that. What nation of
any spirit, thought he, could be expected to stand
such work, paying all her wealth into a foreign treasury and yielding up the flower of her youth under
foreign conscription. It was not so very long ago,

either, since English guns had been heard booming close by in the German Ocean; well—all the fighting was over at last. Holland was a snug little Monarchy now in her own right, and Ben, for one, was glad of it. Arrived at this charitable conclusion, he was prepared to enjoy to the utmost all the wonders of her capital; he quite delighted Mynheer van Gend with his hearty and intelligent interest—so, in fact, did all the boys, for a merrier, more observant party never went sight-seeing.

CHAPTER XXV

THROUGH THE HAGUE

The picture gallery, in Maurits Huis,* one of the finest in the world, seemed only to have flashed by the boys during a two hours' visit, so much was there to admire and examine. As for the Royal Cabinet of curiosities, in the same building, they felt that they had but glanced at it though they were there nearly half a day. It seemed to them that Japan had poured all her treasures within its walls. For a long period, Holland, always foremost in commerce, was the only nation allowed to have any intercourse with Japan. One can well forego a journey to that country if he can but visit the Museum at the Hague.

Room after room is filled with collections from the Hermit Empire—Costumes peculiar to various ranks and pursuits, articles of ornament, household utensils, weapons, armor and surgical instruments. There is also an ingenious Japanese model of the island of Desina, the Dutch factory in Japan. It appears almost as the Island itself would if seen through a reversed opera-glass, and makes one feel like a Gulliver coming unexpectedly upon a Japanese Lilliput. There you see hundreds of people in native costumes, standing, kneeling, stooping, reaching— all at work, or pretending to be—and their dwellings, even their very furniture, spread out before you, plain as day. In another room a huge tortoise shell baby-house fitted up in Dutch style and inhabited by dignified Dutch dolls, stands ready to tell you at a glance how people live in Holland.

Gretel, Hilda, Katrinka, even the proud Rychie

*A building erected by Prince Maurice of Nassau.

Korbes, would have been delighted with this; but
Peter and his gallant band passed it by without a
glance. The war implements had the honor of de-
taining them for an hour; such clubs, such murder-
ous krits, or daggers, such firearms, and, above all,
such wonderful Japanese swords, quite capable of
performing the accredited Japanese feat of cutting
a man in two at a single stroke!

There were Chinese and other oriental curiosities
in the collection. Native historical relics, too, upon
which our young Dutchmen gazed very soberly,
though they were secretly proud to show them to
Ben.

There was a model of the cabin at Saardam in
which Peter the Great lived during his short career
as a ship-builder. Also, wallets and bowls—once
carried by the "Beggar" Confederates who, uniting
under the Prince of Orange, had freed Holland from
the tyranny of Spain; the sword of Admiral Van
Speyk who about ten years before had perished in
voluntarily blowing up his own ship; and Van
Tromp's armor with the marks of bullets upon it.
Jacob looked around, hoping to see the broom
which the plucky admiral fastened to his mast-head
—but it was not there. The waistcoat which William Third* of England wore during the last days
of his life, possessed great interest for Ben; and
one and all gazed with a mixture of reverence and
horror-worship at the identical clothing worn by
William the Silent* when he was murdered at Delft
by Balthazar Geraerts. A tawny leather doublet
and plain surcoat of gray cloth, a soft felt hat, and
a high neck-ruff from which hung one of the "Beg-

*William, Prince of Orange, who became King of England,
was a great grandson of William the Silent, Prince of Orange,
who was murdered by Geraerts (or Gerard) July 10th, 1584.

gars' " medals—these were not in themselves very
princely objects, though the doublet had a tragic
interest from its dark stains and bullet holes. Ben
could readily believe, as he looked upon the garments, that the Silent Prince, true to his greatness
of character, had been exceedingly simple in his
attire. His aristocratic prejudices were, however,
decidedly shocked when Lambert told him of the way
in which William's bride first entered the Hague.

"The beautiful Louisa de Coligny, whose father
and former husband both had fallen at the Massacre
of St. Bartholomew, was coming to be fourth wife
to the Prince, and of course," said Lambert, "we
Hollanders were too gallant to allow the lady to
enter the town on foot. No, sir, we sent (or rather
my ancestors did) a clean open post-wagon to meet
her, with a plank across it for her to sit upon!"

"Very gallant indeed!" exclaimed Ben with almost
a sneer in his polite laugh—"and she the daughter
of an Admiral of France."

"Was she? Upon my word I had nearly forgotten
that. But, you see Holland had very plain ways in
the good old time, in fact we are a very simple,
frugal people to this day. The Van Gend establishment is a decided exception, you know."

"A very agreeable exception, I think," said Ben.

"Certainly, certainly. But, between you and me,
Mynheer van Gend, though he has wrought his own
fortunes, can afford to be magnificent, and yet be
frugal."

"Exactly so," said Ben profoundly; at the same
time stroking his upper lip and chin, which latterly
he believed had been showing delightful and unmis-
takable signs of coming dignities.

While tramping on foot through the city, Ben
often longed for a good English sidewalk. Here,

as in the other towns, there was no curb, no raised
pavement for foot travelers—but the streets were
clean and even, and all vehicles were kept scrupu-
lously within a certain tract. Strange to say, there
were nearly as many sleds as wagons to be seen,
though there was not a particle of snow. The sleds
went scraping over the bricks or cobblestones; some
provided with an apparatus in front for sprinkling
water, to diminish the friction, and some rendered
less musical by means of a dripping oil rag, which
the driver occasionally applied to the runners.

Ben was surprised at the noiseless way in which
Dutch laborers do their work. Even around the
warehouses and docks there was no bustle, no shouting from one to another. A certain twitch of the
pipe, or turn of the head or, at most, a raising of the
hand, seemed to be all the signal necessary. Entire
loads of cheeses or herrings are pitched from cart or
canal-boat into the warehouses without a word; but
the passer-by must take his chance of being pelted,
for a Dutchman seldom looks before or behind him
while engaged at work.

Poor Jacob Poot, who seemed destined to bear all
the mishaps of the journey, was knocked nearly
breathless by a great cheese, which a fat Dutchman
was throwing to a fellow-laborer; but he recovered
himself, and passed on without evincing the least
indignation.

Ben professed great sympathy on the occasion,
but Jacob insisted that it was "notting."

"Then why did you screw your face so when it
hit you?"

"What for screw mine face," repeated Jacob soberly, "vy, it vash de—de—"

"The what?" insisted Ben, maliciously.

"Vy, de—de—vat you call dis, vat you taste mit de nose?"

Ben laughed.

"Oh, you mean the smell."

"Yesh. Dat ish it," said Jacob eagerly—"it wash de schmell. I draw mine face for dat!"

"Ha! ha!" roared Ben, "that's a good one. A Dutch boy smell a cheese. You can never make me believe that!"

"Vell, it is no matter," replied Jacob, trudging on beside Ben in perfect good humor—"vait till you hit mit cheese—dat ish all."

Soon he added pathetically—"Penchamin, I no likes be called Tutch—dat ish no goot. I bees a Hollander."

Just as Ben was apologizing Lambert hailed him.

"Hold up! Ben. Here is the Fish Market. There is not much to be seen at this season. But we can take a look at the storks if you wish."

Ben knew that storks were held in peculiar reverence in Holland, and that the bird figured upon the arms of the Capitol. He had noticed cart-wheels placed upon the roofs of Dutch cottages, to entice storks to settle upon them; he had seen their huge nests, too, on many a thatched gable roof from Broek to the Hague. But it was Winter now. The nests were empty. No greedy birdlings opened their mouths—or rather their heads—at the approach of a great white winged thing, with outstretched neck and legs, bearing a dangling something for their breakfast. The long bills were far away, picking up food on African shores; and before they would return in the Spring, Ben's visit to the land of dikes would be over.

Therefore he pressed eagerly forward, as Van Mounen led the way through the fish-market, anx-

ious to see if storks in Holland were anything like
the melancholy specimens he had seen in the Zoo-
logical Gardens of London.

It was the same old story. A tamed bird is a
sad bird, say what you will. These storks lived in
a sort of kennel, chained by the feet like felons,
though supposed to be honored by being kept at the
public expense. In Summer they were allowed to
walk about the market, where the fish-stalls were
like so many free dining-saloons to them. Untasted
delicacies in the form of raw fish and butcher's
offals, lay about their kennels now, but the city-
guests preferred to stand upon one leg, curving back
their long necks and leaning their heads sidewise, in
a blinking reverie. How gladly they would have
changed their petted state for the busy life of some
hard-working stork mother, or father, bringing up a
troublesome family on the roof of a rickety old
building, where flapping windmills frightened them
half to death every time they ventured forth on a
frolic.

Ben soon made up his mind, and rightly, too, that
the Hague with its fine streets and public parks
shaded with elms, was a magnificent city. The pre-
vailing costume was like that of London or Paris,
and his British ears were many a time cheered by
the music of British words. The shops were different in many respects from those on Oxford Street
and the Strand, but they often were illumined by
a printed announcement that English was "spoken
within." Others proclaimed themselves to have
London Stout for sale—and one actually promised
to regale its customers with ENGLISH ROAST BEEF.

Over every possible shop-door was the never-fail-
ing placard, "Tabak te Koop" (tobacco to be sold).
Instead of colored glass globes in the windows, or

high jars of leeches, the drug-stores had a gaping
Turk's head at the entrance—or, if the establishment were particularly fine, a wooden mandarin entire, indulging in a full yawn.

Some of these queer faces amused Ben exceedingly; they seemed to have just swallowed a dose
of physic; but Van Mounen declared he could not
see anything funny about them. A druggist showed
his sense by putting a *Gaper* before his door, so
that his place could be known at once as an "apoth-
eek" and that was all there was about it.

Another thing attracted Ben—the milkmen's
carts. These were small affairs, filled with shiny
brass kettles, or some jars, and drawn by dogs.
The milkmen walked meekly beside his cart, keeping
his dog in order, and delivering the milk to customers. Certain fish dealers had dog-carts, also,
and when a herring-dog chanced to meet a milk-dog
he invariably put on airs and growled as he passed
him. Sometimes a milk-dog would recognize an
acquaintance before another milk-cart across the
street, and then how the kettles would rattle, especially if they were empty! Each dog would give a
bound and, never caring for his master's whistle,
insist upon meeting the other halfway. Sometimes
they contented themselves with an inquisitive sniff,
but, generally the smaller dog made an affectionate
snap at the larger one's ear, or a friendly tussle
was engaged in by way of exercise. Then woe! to
the milk kettles, and woe! to the dogs!

The whipping over, each dog, expressing his feelings as best he could, would trot leisurely back to
his work.

If some of these animals were eccentric in their
ways, others were remarkably well-behaved. In
fact, there was a school for dogs in the city, estab-

lished expressly for training them; Ben probably
saw some of its graduates. Many a time he noticed
a span of barkers trotting along the street with
all the dignity of horses, obeying the slightest hint
of the man walking briskly beside them. Sometimes, when their load was delivered, the dealer
would jump in the cart, and have a fine drive to his
home beyond the gates of the city; and sometimes,
I regret to say, a patient vrouw would trudge beside the cart, with fish-basket upon her head, and a
child in her arms—while her lord enjoyed his drive,
carrying no heavier burden than a stumpy clay pipe,
the smoke of which mounted lovingly into her face.

CHAPTER XXVI

A DAY OF REST

The sight seeing came to an end at last, and so did our boys' visit to the Hague. They had spent three happy days and nights with the Van Gends, and, strange to say, had not once, in all that time, put on skates. The third day had indeed been one of rest. The noise and bustle of the city was hushed; sweet Sunday bells sent blessed, tranquil thoughts into their hearts. Ben felt, as he listened to their familiar music, that the Christian world is one, after all, however divided by sects and differences it may be. As the clock speaks everyone's native language in whatever land it may strike the hour, so church bells are never foreign if our hearts but listen.

Led on by those clear voices, our party, with Mevrouw van Gend and her husband, trod the quiet but crowded streets, until they came to a fine old church in the southern part of the city.

The interior was large and, notwithstanding its great stained windows, seemed dimly lighted, though the walls were white and dashes of red and purple sunshine lay brightly upon pillar and pew.

Ben saw a few old women softly moving through the aisles, each bearing a high pile of foot-stoves which she distributed among the congregation by skillfully slipping out the under one, until none were left. It puzzled him that mynheer should settle himself with the boys in a comfortable side-pew, after seating his vrouw in the body of the church, which was filled with chairs exclusively appropriate to the women. But Ben was learning only a common custom of the country.

The pews of the nobility and the dignitaries of
the city were circular in form, each surrounding a
column. Elaborately carved, they formed a massive
base to their great pillars standing out in bold relief
against the blank, white walls beyond. These columns, lofty and well-proportioned were nicked and
defaced from violence done to them long ago; yet
it seemed quite fitting that, before they were lost
in the deep arches overhead, their softened outlines
should leaf out as they did into richness and beauty.

Soon, Ben lowered his gaze to the marble floor. It
was a pavement of grave-stones. Nearly all the
large slabs, of which it was composed, marked the
restingplaces of the dead. An armorial design engraved upon each stone, with inscription and date,
told whose form was sleeping beneath, and sometimes three of a family were lying one above the
other in the same sepulcher

He could not but think of the solemn funeral pro-
cession winding by torch-light through those lofty
aisles, and bearing its silent burden toward a dark
opening whence a slab had been lifted, in readiness
for its coming. It was something to feel that his
sister Mabel, who died in her flower, was lying in
a sunny church-yard, where a brook rippled and
sparkled in the day-light, and waving trees whispered together all night long; where flowers might
nestle close to the headstone and moon and stars
shed their peace upon it, and mourning birds sing
sweetly overhead.

Then he looked up from the pavement and rested
his eyes upon the carved, oaken pulpit, exquisitely
beautiful in design and workmanship. He could
not see the minister—though, not long before, he
had watched him slowly ascending its winding stair

—a mild-faced man wearing a ruff about his neck, and a short cloak reaching nearly to the knees.

Meantime the great church had been silently filling. Its pews were somber with men and its center radiant with women in their fresh Sunday attire. Suddenly a soft rustling spread through the building All eyes were turned toward the minister now appearing above the pulpit.

Although the sermon was spoken slowly, Ben could understand little of what was said; but when the hymn came, he joined in with all his heart. A thousand voices lifted in love and praise offered a grander language than he could readily comprehend.

Once he was startled, during a pause in the service, by seeing a little bag suddenly shaken before him. It had a tinkling bell at its side, and was attached to a long stick carried by one of the deacons of the church Not relying solely upon the mute appeal of the poor-boxes fastened to the columns near the entrance, this more direct method was resorted to, of awakening the sympathies of the charitable.

Fortunately Ben had provided himself with a few stivers, or the musical bag must have tinkled before him in vain.

More than once, a dark look rose on our English boy's face that morning. He longed to stand up and harangue the people concerning a peculiarity that filled him with pain. Some of the men wore their hats during the service, or took them off whenever the humor prompted, and many put theirs on in the church as soon as they arose to leave. No wonder Ben's sense of propriety was wounded; and yet a higher sense would have been exercised had he tried to feel willing that Hollanders should fol-

low the customs of their country But his English
heart said over and over again, "It is outrageous!
It is sinful!"

There is an Angel called Charity who often would
save our hearts a great deal of trouble if we would
but let her in.

CHAPTER XXVII

HOMEWARD BOUND

On Monday morning, bright and early, our boys bade farewell to their kind entertainers and started on their homeward journey.

Peter lingered awhile at the lion-guarded door, for he and his sister had many parting words to say.

As Ben saw them bidding each other "good-bye," he could not help feeling that kisses as well as clocks were wonderfully alike everywhere. The English kiss that his sister Jennie gave when he left home had said the same thing to him that the Vrouw van Gend's Dutch kiss said to Peter. Ludwig had taken his share of the farewell in the most matter-of-fact manner possible, and though he loved his sister well, had winced a little at her making such a child of him as to put an extra kiss "for mother" upon his forehead.

He was already upon the canal with Carl and Jacob. Were they thinking about sisters or kisses? Not a bit of it. They were so happy to be on skates once more, so impatient to dart at once into the very heart of Broek, that they spun and wheeled about like crazy fellows, relieving themselves meantime, by muttering something about "Peter and donder" not worth translating.

Even Lambert and Ben who had been waiting at the street-corner began to grow impatient.

The captain joined them at last; they were soon on the canal with the rest.

"Hurry up, Peter," growled Ludwig—"we're freezing by inches—there! I knew you'd be the last after all to get on your skates!"

"Did you?" said his brother looking up with an air of deep interest—"clever boy!"

Ludwig laughed, but tried to look cross, as he said —"I'm in earnest, anyhow. We must get home some time this year."

"Now, boys," cried Peter springing up, as he fastened the last buckle. "There's a clear way before us! We will imagine it's the grand race. Ready! One—two—three—START!"

I assure you very little was said for the first half hour. They were six Mercuries skimming the ice. In plain English they went like lightning—no, that is imaginary too. The fact is, one cannot decide what to say when half a dozen boys are whizzing past at such a rate. I can only tell you that each did his best, flying, with bent body, and eager eyes, in and out among the placid skaters on the canal, until the very guard shouted to them to "hold up!" This only served to send them onward with a two-boy power that startled all beholders.

But the laws of inertia are stronger even than canal-guards.

After a while Jacob slackened his speed—then Ludwig—then Lambert—then Carl.

They soon halted to take a long breath, and, finally found themselves standing in a group gazing after Peter and Ben who were still racing in the distance as if their lives were at stake.

"It is very evident," said Lambert, as he and his three companions started on again, "that neither of them will give up until he can't help it."

"What foolishness!" growled Carl, "to tire themselves at the beginning of the journey—but they're racing in earnest—that's certain. Hallo! Peter's flagging!"

"Not so!" cried Ludwig—"catch him being beaten!"

"Ha! ha!" sneered Carl. "I tell you, boy, Benjamin is ahead."

Now if Ludwig disliked anything in this world, it was to be called a boy—probably because he was nothing else. He grew indignant at once.

"Humph, what are you, I wonder. There, sir! now look and see if Peter isn't ahead!"

"I think he is," interposed Lambert, "but I can't quite tell at this distance."

"I think he isn't!" retorted Carl.

Jacob was growing anxious—he always abhorred an argument—so he said in a coaxing tone—"Don't quarrel—don't quarrel!"

"Don't quarrel!" mocked Carl, looking back at Jacob as he skated. "Who's quarreling? Poot, you're a goose!"

"I can't help that," was Jacob's meek reply. "See! they are nearing the turn of the canal."

"Now we can see!" cried Ludwig in great excitement.

"Peter will make it first, I know."

"He can't—for Ben is ahead!" insisted Carl. "Gunst! That ice-boat will run over him. No! he is clear! They're a couple of geese anyhow. Hurrah! they're at the turn. Who's ahead?"

"Peter!" cried Ludwig, joyfully.

"Good for the captain!" shouted Lambert and Jacob.

And Carl condescended to mutter:

"It is Peter after all. I thought, all the time, that head fellow was Ben."

This turn in the canal had evidently been their goal, for the two racers came to a sudden halt after passing it.

Carl said something about being glad that they had "sense enough to stop and rest,"—and the four boys skated on in silence to overtake their companions.

All the while, Carl was secretly wishing that he had kept on with Peter and Ben, as he felt sure he could easily have come out winner. He was a very rapid, though by no means a graceful skater.

Ben was looking at Peter with mingled vexation, admiration and surprise, as the boys drew near.

They heard him saying in English:

"You're a perfect bird on the ice, Peter van Holp. The first fellow that ever beat me in a fair race, I can tell you!"

Peter, who understood the language better than he could speak it, returned a laughing bow at Ben's compliment, but made no further reply. Possibly he was scant of breath at the time.

"Now, Penchamin, vat you do mit yourself? get so hot as a fire-brick—dat ish no goot," was Jacob's plaintive comment.

"Nonsense!" answered Ben. "This frosty air will cool me soon enough. I am not tired."

"You are beaten, though, my boy," said Lambert in English, "and fairly, too. How will it be, I wonder, on the day of the grand race?"

Ben flushed, and gave a proud, defiant laugh, as if to say:

"This was mere pastime. I'm determined to beat them—come what will!"

CHAPTER XXVIII

BOYS AND GIRLS

By the time the boys reached the village of Voorhout, which stands near the grand canal, about half way between the Hague and Haarlem, they were forced to hold a council. The wind, though moderate at first, had grown stronger and stronger, until at last they could hardly skate against it. The weather-vanes throughout the country had evidently entered into a conspiracy.

"No use trying to face such a blow as this," said Ludwig. "It cuts its way down a man's throat like a knife."

"Keep your mouth shut, then," grunted the affable Carl, who was strong-chested as a young ox, "I'm for keeping on."

"In this case," interposed Peter, "we must consult the weakest of the party rather than the strongest."

The captain's principle was all right, but its application was not flattering to Master Ludwig; shrugging his shoulders, he retorted:

"Who's weak? Not I, for one—but the wind's stronger than any of us. I hope you'll condescend to admit that!"

"Ha! ha!" laughed Van Mounen, who could barely keep his feet, "so it is."

Just then the weather-vanes telegraphed to each other by a peculiar twitch—and, in an instant, the gust came. It nearly threw the strong-chested Carl; it almost strangled Jacob; and quite upset Ludwig.

"This settles the question," shouted Peter, "off with your skates! We'll go into Voorhout."

At Voorhout they found a little inn with a big

yard. The yard was well bricked, and better than all, was provided with a complete set of skittles, so our boys soon turned the detention into a frolic. The wind was troublesome even in that sheltered quarter, but they were on good standing-ground— and did not mind it.

First a hearty dinner—then a game. With pins as long as their arms, and balls as big as their heads, plenty of strength left for rolling, and a clean sweep of sixty yards for the strokes—no wonder they were happy.

That night Captain Peter and his men slept soundly. No prowling robber came to disturb them, and, as they were distributed in separate rooms, they did not even have a bolster-battle in the morning.

Such a breakfast as they ate! The landlord looked frightened. When he had asked them where they "belonged," he made up his mind that the Broek people starved their children. It was a shame, "such fine young gentlemen, too!"

Fortunately the wind had tired itself out, and fallen asleep in the great sea-cradle beyond the Dunes. There were signs of snow; otherwise, the weather was fine.

It was mere child's-play for the well-rested boys to skate to Leyden. Here they halted awhile, for Peter had an errand at the "Golden Eagle." He left the city with a lightened heart; Dr. Boekman had been at the hotel, read the note containing Hans' message, and departed for Broek.

"I cannot say it was your letter sent him off so soon," explained the landlord, "some rich lady in Broek was taken bad very sudden, and he was sent for in haste."

Peter turned pale.

"What was the name?" he asked.

"Indeed, it went in one ear, and out of the other—for all I hindered it. Plague to people who can't see a traveler in comfortable lodgings, but they must whisk him off, before one can breathe."

"A lady in Broek, did you say?"

"Yes," very gruffly, "any other business, young master?"

"No, mine host—except that I and my comrades here would like a bite of something, and a drink of hot coffee."

"Ah," said the landlord, sweetly, "a bite you shall have, and coffee too, the finest in Leyden. Walk up to the stove, my masters—now I think again—that was a widow lady—from Rotterdam, I think they said—visiting at one Van Stoepel's if I mistake not."

"Ah!" said Peter, greatly relieved. "They live in the white house by the Schlossen Mill—now, mynheer, the coffee, please!"

"What a goose I was," thought he, as the party left the Golden Eagle, "to feel so sure it was my mother—but she may be somebody's mother, poor woman, for all that. Who can she be, I wonder?"

There were not many upon the canal that day, between Leyden and Haarlem. However, as the boys neared Amsterdam, they found themselves once more in the midst of a moving throng. The big *Ysbreeker,** had been at work for the first time that season, but there was any amount of skating ground left yet.

"Three cheers for home!" cried Van Mounen, as they came in sight of the great Western dock (Westelijk Dok). "Hurrah! Hurrah!" shouted one and all, "Hurrah! Hurrah!"

This trick of cheering was an importation among

*Ice-breaker—A heavy machine armed with iron spikes for breaking the ice as it is dragged along.

our party. Lambert van Mounen had brought it
from England. As they always gave it in English,
it was considered quite an exploit and, when circumstances permitted, always enthusiastically performed, to the sore dismay of their quiet-loving
countrymen.

Therefore, their arrival at Amsterdam created
a great sensation, especially among the small boys
on the wharf.

The Y was crossed. They were on the Broek
canal.

Lambert's home was reached first.

"Good-bye, boys!" he cried, as he left them, "we've
had the greatest frolic ever known in Holland."

"So we have. Good-bye, Van Mounen!" answered
the boys.

"Good-bye!"

Peter hailed him. "I say, Van Mounen, the classes
begin to-morrow!"

"I know it. Our holiday is over. Good-bye,
again."

"Good-bye!"

Broek came in sight. Such meetings! Katrinka
was on the canal! Carl was delighted. Hilda was
there! Peter felt rested in an instant. Rychie was
there! Ludwig and Jacob nearly knocked each other
over in their eagerness to shake hands with her.

Dutch girls are modest and generally quiet; but
they have very glad eyes. For a few moments, it
was hard to decide whether Hilda, Rychie or Katrinka felt the most happy.

Annie Bouman was also on the canal, looking
even prettier than the other maidens in her graceful
peasant's costume. But she did not mingle with
Rychie's party; neither did she look unusually
happy.

The one she liked most to see was not among the
new comers.   Indeed he was not upon the canal at
all.   She had not been near Broek before, since the
Eve of St. Nicholas, for she was staying with her
sick grandmother in Amsterdam, and had been
granted a brief resting-spell, as the grandmother
called it, because she had been such a faithful little
nurse night and day.

Annie had devoted her resting-spell to skating
with all her might toward Broek, and back again,
in the hope of meeting her mother or some of her
family on the canal, or, it might be, Gretel Brinker
—not one of them had she seen—and she must hurry
back, without even catching a glimpse of her mother's cottage—for the poor helpless grandmother, she
knew, was by this time moaning for some one to
turn her upon her cot.

Where can Gretel be? thought Annie, as she flew
over the ice, she can almost always steal a few moments from her work, at this time of the day—poor
Gretel—what a dreadful thing it must be to have a
dull father—I should be woefully afraid of him, I
know—so strong, and yet so strange!

Annie had not heard of his illness.   Dame Brinker
and her affairs received but little notice from the
people of the place.

If Gretel had not been known as a goose-girl she
might have had more friends among the peasantry of
the neighborhood.   As it was, Annie Bouman was
the only one who did not feel ashamed to avow
herself by word and deed the companion of Gretel
and Hans.

When the neighbors' children laughed at her for
keeping such poor company, she would simply flush
when Hans was ridiculed, or laugh in a careless, dis-

dainful way; but to hear little Gretel abused always awakened her wrath.

"Goose-girl! indeed!" she would say, "I can tell you any of you are fitter for the work than she. My father often said last Summer that it troubled him to see such a bright-eyed, patient little maiden tending geese. Humph! She would not harm them, as you would, Janzoon Kolp; and she would not tread upon them, as you might, Kate Wouters."

This would be pretty sure to start a laugh at the clumsy, ill-natured Kate's expense; and Annie would walk loftily away from the group of young gossips. Perhaps some memory of Gretel's assailants crossed her mind as she skated rapidly toward Amsterdam, for her eyes sparkled ominously and she more than once gave her pretty head a defiant toss. When that mood passed, such a bright, rosy, affectionate look illumined her face, that more than one weary workingman turned to gaze after her, and to wish that he had a glad, contented lass like that for a daughter.

There were five joyous households in Broek that night.

The boys were back safe and sound; and they found all well at home. Even the sick lady at neighbor Van Stoepel's was out of danger.

But the next morning! Ah, how stupidly schoolbells will ding-dong! ding-dong, when one is tired.

Ludwig was sure he had never listened to anything so odious. Even Peter felt pathetic on the occasion. Carl said it was a shame for a fellow to have to turn out when his bones were splitting—and Jacob soberly bade Ben "Goot Pye!" and walked off with his satchel as if it weighed a hundred pounds.

CHAPTER XXIX

THE CRISIS

While the boys were nursing their fatigue, we will take a peep into the Brinker cottage.

Can it be that Gretel and her mother have not stirred since we saw them last? That the sick man upon the bed has not even turned over? It was four days ago and there is the sad group just as it was before. No, not precisely the same, for Raff Brinker is paler; his fever is gone, though he knows nothing of what is passing. Then, they were alone in the bare, clean room. Now there is another group in an opposite corner.

Dr. Boekman is there, talking in a low tone with a stout young man who listens intently. The stout young man is his student and assistant. Hans is there also. He stands near the window respectfully waiting until he shall be accosted.

"You see, Vollenhoven," said Dr. Boekman, "it is a clear case of"—and here the doctor went off into a queer jumble of Latin and Dutch that I cannot conveniently translate.

After awhile, as Vollenhoven looked at him rather blankly, the learned man condescended to speak to him in simpler phrase.

"It is probably like Rip Donderdunck's case," he exclaimed, in a low, mumbling tone. "He fell from the top of Voppelploot's windmill. After the accident the man was stupid, and finally became idiotic. in time he lay helpless like yon fellow on the bed, moaned, too, like him, and kept constantly lifting his hand to his head. My learned friend Von Choppem performed an operation upon this Donderdunck, and discovered under the skull a small dark sac,

which pressed upon the brain. This had been the
cause of the trouble. My friend Von Choppem re-
moved it—a splendid operation! You see according
to Celsus"—and here the doctor again went off into
Latin.

"Did the man live?" asked the assistant, respectfully.

Dr. Boekman scowled. "That is of no consequence. I believe he died, but why not fix your
mind on the grand features of the case. Consider
a moment how"—and he plunged into Latin mysteries more deeply than ever.

"But, mynheer," gently persisted the student, who
knew that the doctor would not rise to the surface
for hours unless pulled at once from his favorite
depths. "Mynheer, you have other engagements
to-day, three legs in Amsterdam, you remember, and
an eye in Broek, and that tumor up the canal."

"That tumor can wait," said the doctor reflec-
tively. "That is another beautiful case—a beautiful
case! The woman has not lifted her head from her
shoulder for two months—magnificent tumor, sir!"

The doctor by this time was speaking loud. He
had quite forgotten where he was.

Vollenhoven made another attempt.

"This poor fellow on the bed, mynheer. Do you
think you can save him?"

"Ah, indeed, certainly," stammered the doctor,
suddenly perceiving that he had been talking rather
off the point—"certainly, that is—I hope so—"

"If any one in Holland can, mynheer," murmured
the assistant with honest bluntness—"it is yourself."

The doctor looked displeased—growled out a tender request for the student to talk less, and beck-
oned Hans to draw near.

This strange man had a great horror of speaking

to women, especially on surgical matters. "One can never tell," he said, "what moment the creatures will scream or faint." Therefore he explained Raff Brinker's case to Hans and told him what he believed should be done to save the patient.

Hans listened attentively, growing red and pale by turns, and throwing quick, anxious glances toward the bed.

"It may kill the father—did you say, mynheer?" he exclaimed at last, in a trembling whisper.

"It may, my boy. But I have a strong belief that it will cure and not kill. Ah! if boys were not such dunces, I could lay the whole matter before you, but it would be of no use."

Hans looked blank, at this compliment.

"It would be of no use," repeated Doctor Boekman indignantly, "a great operation is proposed—but one might as well do it with a hatchet. The only question asked is—'will it kill?'"

"The question is everything to us, mynheer," said Hans, with tearful dignity.

Doctor Boekman looked at him in sudden dismay.

"Ah! exactly so. You are right, boy, I am a fool. Good boy. One does not wish one's father killed—of course not. I am a fool."

"Will he die, mynheer, if this sickness goes on?"

"Humph! this is no new illness. The same thing growing worse every instant—pressure on the brain —will take him off soon like that," said the doctor, snapping his fingers.

"And the operation may save him," pursued Hans; "how soon, mynheer, can we know?"

Doctor Boekman grew impatient.

"In a day, perhaps an hour. Talk with your mother, boy, and let her decide. My time is short."

Hans approached his mother; at first, when she

looked up at him, he could not utter a syllable; then
turning his eyes away he said in a firm voice:

"I must speak with the mother alone."

Quick little Gretel, who could not quite understand what was passing, threw rather an indignant
look at Hans, and walked away.

"Come back, Gretel, and sit down," said Hans sor-
rowfully.

She obeyed.

Dame Brinker and her boy stood by the window
while the Doctor and his assistant, bending over the
bedside, conversed together in a low tone.   There
was no danger of disturbing the patient.   He appeared like one blind and deaf.   Only his faint, piteous moans showed him to be a living man.   Hans
was talking earnestly, and in a low voice, for he did
not wish his sister to hear.

With dry, parted lips, Dame Brinker leaned
toward him searching his face, as if suspecting a
meaning beyond his words.   Once she gave a quick,
frightened sob that made Gretel start, but, after
that, listened calmly.

When Hans ceased to speak, his mother turned,
gave one long, agonized look at her husband, lying
there so pale and unconscious, and threw herself on
her knees beside the bed.

Poor little Gretel! what did all this mean?   She
looked with questioning eyes at Hans; he was standing, but his head was bent as if in prayer;—at the
Doctor, he was gently feeling her father's head, and
looked like one examining some curious stone;—
at the assistant; the man coughed and turned away;
—at her mother.   Ah! little Gretel, that was the best
you could do—to kneel beside her and twine your
warm, young arms about her neck—to weep and
implore God to listen.

When the mother arose, Doctor Boekman, with a show of trouble in his eyes, asked gruffly, "Well, jufvrouw, shall it be done?"

"Will it pain him, mynheer?" she asked in a trembling voice.

"I cannot say. Probably not. Shall it be done?"

"It may cure him, you said and—mynheer, did you tell my boy that—perhaps—perhaps"—she could not finish.

"Yes, jufvrouw, I said the patient might sink under the operation—but we will hope it may prove otherwise—" he looked at his watch. The assistant moved impatiently toward the window. "Come, jufvrouw, time presses. Yes, or no?"

Hans wound his arm about his mother. It was not his usual way. He even leaned his head against her shoulder.

"The meester awaits an answer," he whispered.

Dame Brinker had long been the head of her house in every sense—many a time she had been very stern with Hans, ruling him with a strong hand, and rejoicing in her motherly discipline—now she felt so weak, so helpless. It was something to feel that firm embrace. There was strength even in the touch of that yellow hair.

She turned to her boy imploringly.

"Oh, Hans! What shall I say?"

"Say what God tells thee, mother," answered Hans, bowing his head.

One quick, questioning prayer to Heaven rose from the mother's heart. The answer came.

She turned toward Doctor Boekman.

"It is right, mynheer. I consent."

"Humph!" grunted the doctor, as if to say, "you've been long enough about it." Then he conferred a moment with his assistant, who listened with great

outward deference but was inwardly rejoicing at
the grand joke he would have to tell his fellow students. He had actually seen a tear in "old Boekman's" eye.

Meanwhile Gretel looked on in trembling silence—
but when she saw the doctor open a leathern case,
and take out one sharp instrument after another,
she sprang forward.

"Oh, mother—the poor father meant no wrong.
Are they going to murder him?"

"I do not know, child," screamed Dame Brinker,
looking fiercely at Gretel. "I DO NOT KNOW."

"This will not do, jufvrouw," said Dr. Boekman
sternly, and at the same time he cast a quick, pene-
trating look at Hans—"you and the girl must leave
the room. The boy may stay."

Dame Brinker drew herself up in an instant. Her
eyes flashed. Her whole countenance was changed.
She looked like one who had never wept, never felt
a moment's weakness. Her voice was low but decided. "I stay with my husband, mynheer."

Dr. Boekman looked astonished. His orders were
seldom disregarded in this style. For an instant his
eye met hers.

"You may remain, jufvrouw," he said in an
altered voice.

Gretel had already disappeared.

In one corner of the cottage was a small closet
where her rough, box-like bed was fastened against
the wall: none would think of the trembling little
creature crouching there in the dark.

Dr. Boekman took off his heavy coat; he filled an
earthen basin with water and placed it near the bed.
Then turning to Hans he asked:

"Can I depend upon you, boy?"

"You can, mynheer."

"I believe you. Stand at the head, here—your mother may sit at your right—so," and he placed a chair near the cot.

"Remember, jufvrouw, there must be no cries, no fainting."

Dame Brinker answered him with a look.

He was satisfied.

"Now, Vollenhoven."

Oh! that case with the terrible instruments. The assistant lifted them. Gretel, who had been peering, with brimming eyes, through the crack of the closet door, could remain silent no longer.

She rushed frantically across the apartment, seized her hood, and ran from the cottage.

CHAPTER XXX

GRETEL AND HILDA

It was recess-hour. At the first stroke of the school-house bell, the canal seemed to give a tremendous shout, and grow suddenly alive with boys and girls. The sly thing, shining so quietly under the noonday sun, was a kaleidoscope at heart, and only needed a shake from that great clapper to start it into dazzling changes.

Dozens of gaily clad children were skating in and out among each other, and all their pent-up merriment of the morning was relieving itself in song and shout and laughter. There was nothing to check the flow of frolic. Not a thought of school-books came out with them into the sunshine. Latin, Arithmetic, Grammar, all were locked up for an hour in the dingy school-room. The teacher might be a noun if he wished, and a proper one at that, but they meant to enjoy themselves. As long as the skating was as perfect as this, it made no difference whether Holland were on the North Pole or the Equator; and as for Philosophy, how could they bother themselves about inertia, and gravitation and such things, when it was as much as they could do to keep from getting knocked over in the commotion.

In the height of the fun, one of the children called out:

"What is that?"

"What? Where?" cried a dozen voices.

"Why—don't you see? That dark thing over there by the idiot's cottage."

"I don't see anything," said one.

"I do," shouted another, "it's a dog!"

"Where's any dog?" put in a squeaky voice that

we have heard before—"it's no such thing—it's a heap of rags."

"Pooh! Voost!" retorted another gruffly, "that's about as near the fact as you ever get, it's the goose-girl, Gretel, looking for rats."

"Well, what of it?" squeaked Voost, "isn't she a bundle of rags, I'd like to know?"

"Ha! ha! Pretty good for you, Voost, you'll get a medal for wit yet, if you keep on."

"You'd get something else, if her brother Hans were here. I'll warrant you would!" said a muffled up little fellow with a cold in his head.

As Hans was not there, Voost could afford to scout the insinuation.

"Who cares for him, little sneezer? I'd fight a dozen like him any day, and you in the bargain."

"You would! would you? I'd like to catch you at it," and, by way of proving his words, the sneezer skated off at the top of his speed.

Just then a general chase after three of the biggest boys of the school was proposed,—and friend and foe, frolicsome as ever, were soon united in a common cause.

Only one of all that happy throng remembered the dark little form by the idiot's cottage. Poor, frightened Gretel! She was not thinking of them, though their merry laughter floated lightly toward her, making her feel like one in a dream.

How loud the moans were behind the darkened window—what if those strange men were really killing her father!

The thought made her spring to her feet with a cry of horror!

"Ah! no," she sobbed, sinking upon the frozen mound of earth where she had been sitting, "mother is there, and Hans. They will care for him. But how pale they were. And even Hans was crying!

"Why did the cross old meester keep him, and send me away," she thought, "I could have clung to the mother and kissed her. That always makes her stroke my hair and speak gentle, even after she has scolded me! How quiet it is now! Oh, if the father should die, and Hans, and the mother, what would I do?" and Gretel, shivering with the cold, buried her face in her arms, and cried as if her heart would break.

The poor child had been tasked beyond her strength during the past four days. Through all, she had been her mother's willing little hand-maiden, soothing, helping and cheering the half-widowed woman by day, and watching and praying beside her all the long night. She knew that something terrible and mysterious was taking place at this moment, something that had been too terrible and mysterious for even kind, good Hans to tell.

Then new thoughts came. Why had not Hans told her? It was a shame. It was her father as well as his. She was no baby. She had once taken a sharp knife from the father's hand. She had even drawn him away from the mother on that awful night when Hans, big as he was, could not help her. Why then must she be treated like one who could do nothing? Oh, how very still it was—how bitter, bitter cold! If Annie Bouman had only stayed home instead of going to Amsterdam it wouldn't be so lonely. How cold her feet were growing—was it the moaning that made her feel as if she were floating in the air!

This would not do—the mother might need her help at any moment!

Rousing herself with an effort, Gretel sat upright, rubbing her eyes and wondering—wondering that the sky was so bright and blue—wondering at

the stillness in the cottage—more than all, at the
laughter rising and falling in the distance.

Soon she sank down again, the strange medly of
thought growing more and more confused in her bewildered brain.

What a strange lip the meester had! How the
stork's nest upon the roof seemed to rustle and
whisper down to her? How bright those knives
were, in the leathern case—brighter perhaps than
the silver skates. If she had but worn her new
jacket she would not shiver so. The new jacket was
pretty—the only pretty thing she had ever worn.
God had taken care of her father so long, He would
do it still, if those two men would but go away.
Ah, now the meesters were on the roof, they were
clambering to the top—no—it was her mother and
Hans—or the storks—it was so dark who could tell?
and the mound rocking, swinging in that strange
way. How sweetly the birds were singing. They
must be Winter birds, for the air was thick with
icicles—not one bird—but twenty. Oh! hear them,
mother—wake me, mother, for the race—I am so
tired with crying, and crying—

A firm hand was laid upon her shoulder.

"Get up, little girl!" cried a kind voice. "This
will not do, for you to lie here and freeze."

Gretel slowly raised her head. She was so sleepy
that it seemed nothing strange to her that Hilda
van Gleck should be leaning over her, looking with
kind, beautiful eyes into her face. She had often
dreamed it before.

But she had never dreamed that Hilda was shaking her roughly, almost dragging her by main force
—never dreamed that she heard her saying,
"Gretel! Gretel Brinker! you must awake!"

This was real. Gretel looked up. Still the lovely

delicate young lady was shaking, rubbing, fairly
pounding her. It must be a dream. No, there was
the cottage—and the stork's nest, and the meester's
coach by the canal. She could see them now quite
plainly. Her hands were tingling, her feet throbbing—Hilda was forcing her to walk.

At last Gretel began to feel like herself again.

"I have been asleep," she faltered, rubbing her
eyes with both hands and looking very much
ashamed.

"Yes, indeed, entirely too much asleep," laughed
Hilda, whose lips were very pale, "but you are well
enough now—lean upon me, Gretel; there, keep
moving—you will soon be warm enough to go by
the fire—now let me take you into the cottage."

"Oh, no! no! no! jufvrouw, not in there! the
meester is there. He sent me away!"

Hilda was puzzled, but she wisely forbore to ask
at present for an explanation. "Very well, Gretel
—try to walk faster—I saw you upon the mound
some time ago; but I thought you were playing—
that is right—keep moving."

All this time the kind-hearted girl had been forcing Gretel to walk up and down, supporting her
with one arm, and, with the other, striving as well
as she could to take off her own warm sacque.

Suddenly Gretel suspected her intention.

"Oh, jufvrouw, jufvrouw!" she cried imploringly.
"Please never think of such a thing as that—oh!
please keep it on, I am burning all over, jufvrouw!
I really am burning—not burning exactly—but pins
and needles pricking all over me—oh! jufvrouw,
don't."

The poor child's dismay was so genuine that
Hilda hastened to re-assure her.

"Very well, Gretel, move your arms then — so.

Why, your cheeks are as pink as roses, already. I think the meester will let you in now—he certainly would—is your father so very ill?"

"Ah, jufvrouw," cried Gretel, weeping afresh, "he is dying, I think. There are two meesters in with him at this moment, and the mother has scarce spoken to-day. Can you hear him moan, juf-vrouw?" she added, with sudden terror, "the air buzzes so I cannot hear. He may be dead! oh, I do wish I could hear him!"

Hilda listened. The cottage was very near, but not a sound could be heard.

Something told her that Gretel was right. She ran to the window.

"You cannot see there, my lady," sobbed Gretel, eagerly, "the mother has oiled paper hanging inside. But at the other one, in the south end of the cottage you can look in where the paper is torn."

Hilda in her anxiety ran round, past the corner where the low roof was fringed with its loosened thatch.

A sudden thought checked her.

"It is not right for me to peep into another's house in this way," she said to herself—then softly calling to Gretel, she added, in a whisper, "You may look—perhaps he is only sleeping."

Gretel tried to walk briskly toward the spot, but her limbs were trembling. Hilda hastened to her support.

"You are sick, yourself, I fear," she said kindly.

"No, not sick, jufvrouw—but my heart cries all the time now, even when my eyes are as dry as yours—why! jufvrouw, your eyes are not dry! Are you crying for us? Oh, jufvrouw—if God sees you! Oh, I know father will get better now—" and the little creature, even while reaching to look through the tiny window, kissed Hilda's hand again and again.

The sash was sadly patched and broken, a torn piece of paper hung half way down across it. Gretel's face was pressed to the window.

"Can you see anything?" whispered Hilda at last.

"Yes—the father lies very still, his head is bandaged and all their eyes are fastened upon him. Oh, jufvrouw!" almost screamed Gretel, as she started back, and by a quick, dexterous movement shook off her heavy wooden shoes, "I must go in to my mother! Will you come with me?"

"Not now, the bell is ringing, I shall come again soon. Good-bye!"

Gretel scarce heard the words. She remembered for many a day afterward, the bright, pitying smile on Hilda's face, as she turned away.

CHAPTER XXXI

THE AWAKENING

An angel could not have entered the cottage more noiselessly. Gretel, not daring to look at anyone, slid softly to her mother's side.

The room was very still. She could hear the old doctor breathe. She could almost hear the sparks as they fell into the ashes on the hearth. The mother's hand was very cold, but a burning spot glowed on her cheek; and her eyes were like a deer's—so bright, so sad, so eager.

At last there was a movement upon the bed, very slight, but enough to cause them all to start; Dr. Boekman leaned eagerly forward.

Another movement. The large hand, so white and soft for a poor man's hand, twitched—then raised itself steadily toward the forehead.

It felt the bandage, not in a restless, crazy way, but with a questioning movement, that caused even Dr. Boekman to hold his breath. Then the eyes opened slowly.

'Steady! steady!" said a voice that sounded very strangely to Gretel. "Shift that mat higher, boys! now throw on the clay. The waters are rising fast —no time to—"

Dame Brinker sprang forward like a young panther.

She seized his hands, and leaning over him, cried "Raff! Raff, boy, speak to me!"

"Is it you, Meitje?" he asked faintly—"I have been asleep, hurt, I think—where is little Hans?"

"Here I am, father!" shouted Hans half mad with joy. But the doctor held him back.

"He knows us!" screamed Dame Brinker. "Great God! he knows us! Gretel! Gretel! come, see your father!"

In vain Dr. Boekman commanded "silence" and tried to force them from the bedside. He could not keep them off.

Hans and his mother laughed and cried together, as they hung over the newly-awakened man. Gretel made no sound, but gazed at them all with glad, startled eyes. Her father was speaking in a faint voice.

"Is the baby asleep, Meitje?"

"The baby!" echoed Dame Brinker. "Oh, Gretel! that is you! And he calls Hans 'little Hans.' Ten years asleep! Oh, mynheer, you have saved us all. He has known nothing for ten years! Children, why don't you thank the meester?"

The good woman was beside herself with joy. Dr. Boekman said nothing, but as his eye met hers, he pointed upward. She understood. So did Hans and Gretel.

With one accord they knelt by the cot, side by side. Dame Brinker felt for her husband's hand even while she was praying. Dr. Boekman's head was bowed; the assistant stood by the hearth with his back toward them.

"Why do you pray?" murmured the father, looking feebly from the bed, as they rose. "Is it God's day?"

It was not Sunday; but his vrouw bowed her head —she could not speak.

"Then we should have a chapter," said Raff Brinker, speaking slowly, and with difficulty. "I do not know how it is. I am very, very weak. Mayhap the minister will read to us."

Gretel lifted the big Dutch Bible from its carved shelf.

Dr. Boekman, rather dismayed, handed the Volume to his assistant.

"Read," he muttered, "these people must be kept quiet or the man will die yet."

When the chapter was finished, Dame Brinker motioned mysteriously to the rest by way of telling them that her husband was asleep.

"Now, jufvrouw," said the doctor, in a subdued tone, as he drew on his thick woolen mittens, "there must be perfect quiet. You understand. This is truly a most remarkable case. I shall come again to-morrow. Give the patient no food to-day," and bowing hastily, he left the cottage, followed by his assistant.

His grand coach was not far away; the driver had kept the horses moving slowly up and down by the canal, nearly all the time the doctor had been in the cottage.

Hans went out also.

"May God bless you, mynheer!" he said, blushing and trembling. "I can never repay you, but if—"

"Yes, you can," interrupted the doctor, crossly. "You can use your wits when the patient wakes again. This clacking and sniveling is enough to kill a well man, let alone one lying on the edge of his grave. If you want your father to get well, keep 'em quiet."

So saying, Doctor Boekman, without another word, stalked off to meet his coach, leaving Hans standing there with eyes and mouth wide open.

Hilda was reprimanded severely that day for returning late to school after recess, and for imperfect recitations.

She had remained near the cottage until she heard Dame Brinker laugh, until she had heard Hans say, "Here I am, father!" and then she had gone back to her lessons. What wonder that she missed them! How could she get a long string of Latin verbs by heart, when her heart did not care a fig for them, but would keep saying to itself, "Oh, I am so glad! I am so glad!"

CHAPTER XXXII

BONES AND TONGUES

Bones are strange things. One would suppose that they know nothing at all about school affairs, but they do. Even Jacob Poots' bones, buried as they were in flesh, were sharp in the matter of study hours.

Early on the morning of his return they ached through and through, giving Jacob a twinge at every stroke of the school-bell—as if to say "Stop that clapper! There's trouble in it." After school, on the contrary, they were quiet and comfortable; in fact, seemed to be taking a nap among their cushions.

The other boys' bones behaved in a similar manner—but that is not so remarkable. Being nearer the daylight than Jacob's they might be expected to be more learned in the ways of the world. Master Ludwig's, especially, were like beauty, only skin deep; they were the most knowing bones you ever heard of. Just put before him ever so quietly, a Grammar-book, with a long lesson marked in it, and immediately the sly bone over his eyes would set up such an aching! Request him to go to the garret for your footstove—instantly the bones would remind him that he was "too tired." Ask him to go to the confectioner's a mile away, and presto! not a bone would remember that it ever had been used before.

Bearing all this in mind you will not wonder when I tell you that our five boys were among the happiest of the happy throng pouring forth from the school-house that day.

Peter was in excellent spirits. He had heard

through Hilda of Dame Brinker's laugh and of Hans' joyous words, and he needed no further proof that Raff Brinker was a cured man. In fact the news had gone forth in every direction, for miles around. Persons who had never before cared for the Brinkers, or even mentioned them, except with a contemptuous sneer or a shrug of pretended pity, now became singularly familiar with every point of their history. There was no end to the number of ridiculous stories that were flying about.

Hilda, in the excitement of the moment, had stopped to exchange a word with the doctor's coachman, as he stood by the horses, pommeling his chest and clapping his hands. Her kind heart was overflowing. She could not help pausing to tell the cold, tired-looking man, that she thought the doctor would be out soon; she even hinted to him that she suspected—only suspected—that a wonderful cure had been performed—an idiot brought to his senses. Nay, she was sure of it—for she had heard his widow laugh—no, not his widow, of course, but his wife—for the man was as much alive as anybody, and, for all she knew, sitting up and talking like a lawyer.

All this was very indiscreet. Hilda in an impenitent sort of way felt it to be so.

But it is always so delightful to impart pleasant or surprising news!

She went tripping along by the canal, quite resolved to repeat the sin, *ad infinitum*, and tell nearly every girl and boy in the school.

Meantime, Janzoon Kolp came skating by. Of course in two seconds, he was striking slippery attitudes, and shouting saucy things to the coachman, who stared at him in indolent disdain.

This, to Janzoon, was equivalent to an invitation

to draw nearer. The coachman was now upon his box gathering up the reins and grumbling at his horses.

Janzoon accosted him.

"I say. What's going on at the idiot's cottage? Is your boss in there?"

Coachman nodded mysteriously.

"Whew!" whistled Janzoon, drawing closer. "Old Brinker dead?"

The driver grew big with importance, and silent in proportion.

"See here, old pincushion, I'd run home yonder and get you a chunk of gingerbread if I thought you could open your mouth."

Old pincushion was human—long hours of waiting had made him ravenously hungry. At Janzoon's hint, his countenance showed signs of a collapse.

"That's right, old fellow," pursued his tempter, "hurry up—what news—old Brinker dead?"

"No—cured! got his wits," said the coachman, shooting forth his words, one at a time, like so many bullets.

Like bullets (figuratively speaking), they hit Janzoon Kolp. He jumped as if he had been shot.

"Goede Gunst! you don't say so!"

The man pressed his lips together, and looked significantly toward Master Kolp's shabby residence.

Just then Janzoon saw a group of boys in the distance. Hailing them in a rowdy style, common to boys of his stamp all over the world, whether in Africa, Japan, Amsterdam or Paris—he scampered toward them, forgetting coachman, gingerbread, everything but the wonderful news.

Therefore by sundown it was well known throughout the neighboring country that Dr. Boekman chancing to stop at the cottage had given the idiot

Brinker a tremendous dose of medicine, as brown as gingerbread. It had taken six men to hold him while it was poured down. The idiot had immediately sprung to his feet, in full possession of all his faculties—knocked over the doctor, or thrashed him (there was admitted to be a slight uncertainty as to which of these penalties was inflicted), then sat down and addressed him for all the world like a lawyer. After that he had turned and spoken beautifully to his wife and children. Dame Brinker had laughed herself into violent hysterics. Hans had said, "Here I am, father! your own dear son," and Gretel had said, "Here I am, father, your own dear Gretel!" and the doctor had afterward been seen leaning back in his carriage looking just as white as a corpse.

CHAPTER XXXIII

A NEW ALARM

When Dr. Boekman called the next day at the Brinker cottage, he could not help noticing the cheerful, comfortable aspect of the place, An atmosphere of happiness breathed upon him as he opened the door. Dame Brinker sat complacently knitting beside the bed, her husband was enjoying a tranquil slumber, and Gretel was noiselessly kneading rye-bread on the table in the corner.

The doctor did not remain long. He asked a few simple questions, appeared satisfied with the answers, and after feeling his patient's pulse, said— "Ah, very weak yet, jufvrouw; very weak, indeed. He must have nourishment. You may begin to feed the patient, ahem! not too much, but what you do give him let it be strong and of the best."

"Black bread, we have, mynheer, and porridge," replied Dame Brinker, cheerily, "they have always agreed with him well."

"Tut! tut!" said the doctor, frowning, "nothing of the kind. He must have the juice of fresh meat, white bread, dried and toasted, good Malaga wine, and—ahem; The man looks cold—give him more covering, something light and warm. Where is the boy?"

"Hans, mynheer, has gone into Broek to look for work. He will be back soon. Will the meester please be seated?"

Whether the hard polished stool offered by Dame Brinker did not look particularly tempting, or whether the dame herself frightened him, partly because she was a woman, and partly because an anxious, distressed look had suddenly appeared in her

face, I cannot say. Certain it is that our eccentric
doctor looked hurriedly about him, muttered something about "extraordinary case," bowed, and disappeared, before Dame Brinker had time to say another word.

Strange that the visit of their good benefactor
should have left a cloud, yet so it was. Gretel
frowned, an anxious childish frown, and kneaded
the bread-dough violently, without looking up.
Dame Brinker hurried to her husband's bedside,
leaned over him, and fell into silent but passionate
weeping.

In a moment Hans entered.

"Why, mother," he whispered in alarm, "what
ails thee? Is the father worse?"

She turned her quivering face toward him, making no attempt to conceal her distress.

"Yes. He is starving—perishing. The meester
said it."

Hans turned pale.

"What does this mean, mother? We must feed
him at once. Here, Gretel, give me the porridge."

"Nay!" cried his mother distractedly, yet without
raising her voice, "it may kill him. Our poor fare
is too heavy for him. Oh, Hans, he will die—the
father will die if we use him this way. He must
have meat, and sweet wine, and a dek-bed. Oh,
what shall I do? what shall I do?" she sobbed, ringing her hands. "There is not a stiver in the house."

Gretel pouted; it was the only way she could ex-
press sympathy just then; her tears fell one by one
into the dough.

"Did the meester say he must have these things,
mother?" asked Hans.

"Yes, he did."

"Well, mother, don't cry, he shall have them; I

shall bring meat and wine before night. Take the cover from my bed, I can sleep in the straw."

"Yes, Hans; but it is heavy, scant as it is. The meester said he must have something light and warm. He will perish. Our peat is giving out, Hans. The father has wasted it sorely, throwing it on when I was not looking, dear man."

"Never mind, mother," whispered Hans, cheerfully. "We can cut down the willow tree and burn it, if need be; but I'll bring home something to-night. There must be work in Amsterdam, though there's none in Broek. Never fear, mother; the worst trouble of all is past. We can brave anything now that the father is himself again."

"Aye!" sobbed Dame Brinker, hastily drying her eyes, "that is true indeed."

"Of course it is. Look at him, mother, how softly he sleeps. Do you think God would let him starve, just after giving him back to us. Why, mother, I'm as sure of getting all the father needs, as if my pocket was bursting with gold. There, now, don't fret." And hurriedly kissing her, Hans caught up his skates and skipped from the cottage.

Poor Hans! Disappointed in his morning's errand, half sickened with this new trouble, he wore a brave look, and tried to whistle as he tramped resolutely off with the firm intention of mending matters.

Want had never before pressed as sorely upon the Brinker family. Their stock of peat was nearly exhausted, and all the flour in the cottage was in Gretel's dough. They had scarcely cared to eat during the past few days—scarcely realized their condition. Dame Brinker had felt so sure that she and the children could earn money before the worst came, that she had given herself up to the joy of

her husband's recovery. She had not even told Hans
that the few pieces of silver in the old mitten were
quite gone.

Hans reproached himself, now, that he had not
hailed the doctor when he saw him enter his coach
and drive rapidly away in the direction of Amsterdam.

Perhaps there is some mistake, he thought. The
meester surely would have known that meat and
sweet wine were not at our command; and yet the
father looks weak—he certainly does. I must get
work. If Mynheer van Holp were back from Rotterdam I could get plenty to do. But Master Peter told
me to let him know if he could do aught to serve
us. I shall go to him at once. Oh, if it were but
Summer!"

All this time Hans was hastening towards the
canal. Soon his skates were on, and he was skimming rapidly toward the residence of Mynheer van
Holp.

"The father must have meat and wine at once,"
he muttered, "but how can I earn the money in time
to buy them to-day? There is no other way but to
go, as I promised to Master Peter. What would a
gift of meat and wine be to him? When the father
is once fed, I can rush down to Amsterdam and earn
the morrow's supply."

Then came other thoughts—thoughts that made
his heart thump heavily and his cheeks burn with a
new shame—"It is begging, to say the least. Not
one of the Brinkers has ever been a beggar. Shall
I be the first? Shall my poor father coming back
into life learn that his family have asked for charity—he, always so wise and thrifty? No," cried
Hans aloud, "better a thousand times to part with
the watch."

"I can at least borrow money on it, in Amsterdam!" he thought, turning around, "That will be no disgrace. I can find work at once, and get it back again. Nay, perhaps I can even speak to the father about it!"

This last thought almost made the lad dance for joy.

Why not, indeed, speak to the father. He was a rational being now. "He may wake," thought Hans, "quite bright and rested—may tell us the watch is of no consequence, to sell it of course! Hoezza!" and Hans almost flew over the ice.

A few moments more and the skates were again swinging from his arm. He was running towards the cottage.

His mother met him at the door.

"Oh, Hans!" she cried, her face radiant with joy, "the young lady has been here with her maid. She brought everything—meat, jelly, wine and bread— a whole basketfull! Then the meester sent a man from town with more wine, and a fine bed and blankets for the father.

"Oh! he will get well now. God bless them!"

"God bless them!" echoed Hans, and for the first time that day, his eyes filled with tears.

CHAPTER XXXIV

THE FATHER'S RETURN

That evening Raff Brinker felt so much better that he insisted upon sitting up awhile on the rough, high-backed chair by the fire. For a few moments there was quite a commotion in the little cottage. Hans was all-important on the occasion, for his father was a heavy man, and needed something firm to lean upon. The dame, though none of your fragile ladies, was in such a state of alarm and excitement at the bold step they were taking in lifting him without the meester's orders, that she came near pulling her husband over, even while she believed herself to be his main prop and support.

"Steady, vrouw, steady," painted Raff, "have I grown old and feeble, or is it the fever makes me thus helpless?"

"Hear the man!" laughed Dame Brinker, "talking like any other Christian. Why you're weak from the fever, Raff. Here's the chair, all fixed snug and warm; now, sit thee down—hi-di-didy—there we are!"

With these words, Dame Brinker let her half of the burden settle slowly into the chair. Hans prudently did the same.

Meanwhile Gretel flew about generally, bringing every possible thing to her mother to tuck behind the father's back and spread over his knees. Then she twitched the carved bench under his feet, and Hans kicked the fire to make it brighter.

The father was "sitting up" at last. What wonder that he looked about him like one bewildered. "Little Hans" had just been almost carrying him. "The baby" was over four feet long, and was demurely brushing up the hearth with a bundle of willow wisps. Meitje, the vrouw, winsome and fair as ever, had gained at least fifty pounds in what seemed to him a few hours. She also had some new lines in her face that puzzled him. The only familiar things in the room were the pine table that he had made before he was married, the Bible upon the shelf, and the cupboard in the corner.

Ah! Raff Brinker, it was only natural that your eyes should fill with hot tears even while looking at the joyful faces of your loved ones. Ten years dropped from a man's life are no small loss; ten years of manhood, of household happiness and care; ten years of honest labor, of conscious enjoyment of sunshine and out-door beauty, ten years of grateful life—one day looking forward to all this; the next, waking to find them passed, and a blank. What wonder the scalding tears dropped one by one upon your cheek!

Tender little Gretel! The prayer of her life was answered through those tears. She loved her father from that moment. Hans and his mother glanced silently at each other when they saw her spring toward him, and throw her arms about his neck.

"Father, dear father," she whispered, pressing her cheek close to his, "don't cry. We are all here."

"God bless thee," sobbed Raff, kissing her again and again, "I had forgotten that!"

Soon he looked up again, and spoke in a cheerful voice: "I should know her, vrouw," he said, holding the sweet young face between his hands, and gazing at it as though he were watching it grow. "I should know her. The same blue eyes, and the lips, and, ah! me, the little song she could sing almost before she could stand. But that was long ago," he added, with a sigh, still looking at her dreamily, "long ago, it's all gone now."

"Not so, indeed," cried Dame Brinker, eagerly. "Do you think I would let her forget it? Gretel, child, sing the old song thou hast known so long!"

Raff Brinker's hand fell wearily and his eyes closed, but it was something to see the smile playing about his mouth, as Gretel's voice floated about him like an incense.

It was a simple air; she had never known the words.

With loving instinct she softened every note, until Raff almost fancied that his two-year old baby was once more beside him.

As soon as the song was finished, Hans mounted a wooden stool and began to rummage in the cupboard.

"Have a care, Hans," said Dame Brinker, who through all her poverty was ever a tidy housewife. "Have a care, the wine is there at your right, and the white bread beyond it."

"Never fear, mother," answered Hans, reaching far back upon the upper shelf, "I shall do no mischief."

Jumping down, he walked toward his father, and placed an oblong block of pine-wood in his hands. One of its ends was rounded off, and some deep cuts had been made on the top.

"Do you know what it is, father?" asked Hans.

Raff Brinker's face brightened. "Indeed I do, boy, it is the boat I was making you yest—alack, not yesterday, but years ago."

"I have kept it ever since, father; it can be finished when your hand grows strong again."

"Yes, but not for you, my lad. I must wait for the grandchildren. Why, you are nearly a man.

Have you helped your mother, boy, through all these years?"

"Aye, and bravely," put in Dame Brinker.

"Let me see," muttered the father, looking in a puzzled way at them all, "how long is it since the night when the waters were coming in? 'Tis the last I remember."

"We have told thee true, Raff. It was ten years last Pinxter-week."

"Ten years—and I fell then, you say. Has the fever been on me ever since?"

Dame Brinker scarce knew how to reply. Should she tell him all? Tell him that he had been an idiot, almost a lunatic? The doctor had charged her on no account to worry or excite his patient.

Hans and Gretel looked astonished when the answer came.

"Like enough, Raff," she said, nodding her head, and raising her eyebrows, "when a heavy man like thee falls on his head, it's hard to say what will come—but thou'rt well now, Raff. Thank the good Lord!"

The newly-awakened man bowed his head.

"Aye, well enough, mine vrouw," he said, after a moment's silence, "but my brain somehow turns like a spinning-wheel. It will not be right till I get on the dikes again. When shall I be at work, think you?"

"Hear the man!" cried Dame Brinker delighted, yet frightened, too, for that matter; "we must get him on the bed, Hans. Work indeed!"

They tried to raise him from the chair—but he was not ready yet.

"Be off with ye!" he said, with something like his old smile (Gretel had never seen it before); "does a man want to be lifted about like a log? I tell you before three suns I shall be on the dikes again. Ah! there'll be some stout fellows to greet me. Jan Kamphuisen and young Hoogsvliet. They have been good friends, to thee, Hans, I'll warrant."

Hans looked at his mother. Young Hoogsvliet had been dead five years. Jan Kamphuisen was in the jail at Amsterdam.

"Aye, they'd have done their share no doubt," said Dame Brinker, parrying the inquiry, "had we asked them. But what with working and studying, Hans has been busy enough without seeking comrades."

"Working and studying," echoed Raff, in a musing tone, "can the youngsters read and cipher, Meitje?"

"You should hear them!" she answered proudly, "they can run through a book while I mop the floor. Hans, there, is as happy over a page of big words as a rabbit in a cabbage patch—as for ciphering—"

"Here, lad, help a bit," interrupted Raff Brinker, "I must get me on the bed again."

CHAPTER XXXV

THE THOUSAND GUILDERS

None seeing the humble supper eaten in the Brinker cottage that night, would have dreamed of the dainty fare hidden away near by. Hans and Gretel looked rather wistfully toward the cupboard as they drank their cupful of water and ate their scanty share of black bread; but even in thought they did not rob their father.

After supper, Hans looked so long and earnestly at the ceiling that his mother felt sure she knew of what he was thinking. "Ah!," she said, "I was thinking of the same a while ago—well—it's no blame if we did look to hear something by this time about the thousand guilders. It's plain enough he knows naught about them."

"Thousand guilders," echoed a faint voice from the bed where Raff had been sleeping. "Ah, I am sure they have been of good use to you, vrouw, through the long years while your man was idle."

Hans and his mother hurried to the bedside, as Raff continued: "How long did the money last, Hans? I could not hear what your mother said."

"I said, Raff," stammered Dame Brinker in great distress, "that it was all gone."

"Well, well, wife, do not fret at that; one thousand guilders is not so much for ten years; but it's lucky I told you all about it before I fell."

"Told me what, man?"

"Why, that I had buried the money. In my dream just now, it seemed I had never said aught about it. You know, it was just before daylight on the same day I was hurt. Jan Kamphuisen had said something that made me distrust him, so I rose up that night and buried the money."

"And where did you say you buried the money, father?" said Hans, gently, yet eagerly. "I was only a little one then."

"Close by the willow sapling behind the cottage," said Raff Brinker drowsily, "on the south side of the tree."

And closing his eyes, he fell asleep again.

The moon rose late that night, shining in, full and clear, at the little window. But its beams did not disturb Raff Brinker. He slept soundly, and so did Gretel.

But Hans and his mother had something else to do, and, after a few hurried preparations, they stole forth with a broken spade and a rusty implement that had done many a day's service when Raff was a hale worker on the dikes.

It was so light out of doors they could see the willow distinctly. Quickly they went to it and commenced their work. The frozen ground was as hard as stone, but they were resolute and soon succeeded in making an impression. Then they started to penetrate the soil, but disappointment soon marked their faces as they found no trace of the guilders.

Hour after hour, mother and son worked on. The hole grew larger and deeper. Clouds began to gather in the sky, throwing elfish shadows as they passed. Not until moon and stars faded away and streaks of daylight began to appear, did Meitje Brinker and Hans look hopelessly into each other's face.

They had searched thoroughly, desperately, all round the tree; South, North, East, West. The hidden money was not there!

CHAPTER XXXVI

GLIMPSES

Annie Bouman had a healthy distaste for Janzoon Kolp. Janzoon Kolp, in his own rough way, adored Annie. Annie declared she could not "to save her life" say one civil word to that odious boy. Yet Janzoon believed her to be the sweetest, sauciest creature in the world.

And so it came to pass that the pretty maid would not look up that morning when, skating homeward from Amsterdam, she became convinced that a great burly boy was coming down the canal toward her.

"Humph! if I look at him," thought Annie, "I'll—"

Then she heard a pleasant voice greeting her; and, looking up, she saw not Janzoon but Hans. Hans had been in a hurry, but now, turning with her towards Broek, he told her the good news of his father. Annie was so true a friend that he told her even of their present distress, and of how everything depended upon his obtaining work.

"Good-bye, Annie," he said at last. "The morning is going fast, and I must haste to Amsterdam and sell these skates. Mother must have money at once."

"Sell your new skates, Hans!" cried Annie. "You, the best skater around Broek! Why the Race is coming off in five days!"

"I know it," he answered resolutely. "Good-bye! I shall skate home again on the old wooden ones."

"Then you really are going to sell your new skates if you can find a customer?"

"Of course I am," he replied.

"Well, Hans, if you are going to sell your skates," said Annie, somewhat confused, "well—I know somebody who would like to buy them. You know you won't get half a price for them in Amsterdam. Please give them to me. I'll bring you the money this very afternoon."

Hans found that there was no withstanding Annie when she said "please" and taking off his skates, he said to her:

"I am sorry to be so particular, but if your friend should not want them, will you bring them back to me to-day? I must buy peat and meal for mother early to-morrow morning."

"My friend will want them," laughed Annie, nodding gaily, and skating off at the top of her speed.

As Hans drew forth the wooden "runners" from his capacious pockets and fastened them on as best he could, he did not hear Annie murmur, "I wish I had not been so rude; poor, brave Hans; what a noble boy he is!" And as Annie skated homeward filled with pleasant thoughts, she did not hear Hans say, "I grumbled like a bear—but bless her! some girls are like angels!"

Perhaps it was all for the best. One cannot be expected to know everything that is going on in the world.

CHAPTER XXXVII

LOOKING FOR WORK

Luxuries unfit us for returning to hardships easily endured before. The wooden runners squeaked more than ever. It was as much as Hans could do to get on with the clumsy old things; still he did not regret that he had parted with his beautiful skates—but resolutely pushed back the boyish trouble that he had not been able to keep them just a little longer, at least until after the race.

That day Hans went up and down the streets of Amsterdam looking for work. He succeeded in earning a few stivers by assisting a man who was driving a train of loaded mules into the city, but he could obtain steady employment nowhere. In the shops and the factories he always met with the same answer; and toward sunset he started on his return to Broek, uncertain whether the strange, choking sensation in his throat arose from discouragement or resolution. There was certainly one more chance. Mynheer Van Holp might have returned by this time. Master Peter, it was reported, had gone to Haarlem the night before to attend to something connected with the great Skating Race. Still Hans would go and try.

Fortunately, Peter had returned early that morning. He was at home when Hans reached there, and was just about to start for the Brinker cottage.

"Ah, Hans!" he cried. "You are the very one I wished to see. Come in and warm yourself."

A short time later Hans left the Van Holp mansion with a lightened heart. Peter had brought word from Haarlem—he had actually gone there to make this plan with his father—that young Brinker was to commence working upon the summer-house doors immediately. There was a comfortable workshop on the place and it was to be at his service until the carving was done.

Before they parted, however, Peter advised Hans to keep himself in good skating condition.

"I shall not be in the race, mynheer," said Hans, looking down.

"Not be in the race! Why not indeed?" and immediately Peter's thoughts swept on a full tide of suspicion towards Carl Schummel.

"Because I cannot, mynheer," answered Hans.

Something in the boy's manner warned Peter that it would be no kindness to press the matter further. He bade Hans "good-bye" and stood thoughtfully watching him as he walked away.

But Peter's thoughtful look changed to a look of puzzled surprise when he saw Hans kneel down by the canal and put on the wooden skates.

"Very queer," muttered Peter, shaking his head as he turned to go into the house, "why in the world doesn't the boy wear his new ones?"

CHAPTER XXXVIII

THE FAIRY GODMOTHER

The sun had gone down quite out of sight when our hero—with a happy heart but with something like a sneer on his countenance, as he jerked off the wooden "runners"—trudged hopefully toward the tiny hut-like building, known of old as the Idiot's cottage.

Duller eyes than his would have discerned two slight figures moving near the door-way, and he soon saw that they were Gretel and Annie. With a joyous shout, he hastened towards them.

"Huzza, girls, I've found work!"

His mother came to the cottage door to hear the good news; then Annie, drawing Hans aside, whispered, "Your skates are sold and here's the money."

"Seven guilders!" cried Hans, "why that is three times as much as I paid for them."

"I cannot help that," said Annie. "If the buyer knew no better, it is not your fault."

"Now, Annie, I know you would never mean that! You must return some of this money."

"But I'll not do any such thing," insisted Annie. "They're sold, and that's an end of it."

Dame Brinker was delighted at the sight of so much silver, but when she learned that Hans had parted with his treasures to obtain it, she sighed, as she exclaimed:

"Bless thee, child! That will be a sore loss for thee!"

Called inside for a moment by her husband, Dame Brinker came out again within a few minutes to find Hans and Gretel standing before Annie, who was seated carelessly on a stump back of the cottage.

"That is as good as a picture," cried she. "Many a

painting have I seen at the grand house at Heidelberg not a whit prettier. My two are rough chubs, Annie, but you look like a fairy."

"Do I," laughed Annie. "Well, then Gretel and Hans, imagine I'm your godmother just paying you a visit. Now I'll grant you each a wish. What will you have, Master Hans?"

A shade of earnestness passed over Annie's face as she looked up at him, and something whispered to Hans that for the moment she was more than mortal.

"I wish," said he, solemnly, "I could find something I was searching for last night."

Gretel laughed merrily. Dame Brinker moaned, "Shame on you, Hans!" and passed wearily into the cottage.

The fairy godmother sprang up and stamped her foot three times.

"Thou shalt have thy wish," she said, "let them say what they will." Then with playful solemnity, she put her hand in her apron pocket and drew forth a large glass bead. "Bury this," said she, giving it to Hans, "where I have stamped, and ere moonrise, thy wish shall be granted."

Then she called out, "Good-night, mortals!" and ran quickly homeward.

All in an instant Hans plunged into the cottage, came out again bearing the spade, and cried to his sister, "I am going to bury my magic bead!"

Raff Brinker slept soundly; his wife took a small block of peat from her small store, and put it on the embers. Then opening the door, she called gently:

"Come in, children."

"Mother, mother! See here!" shouted Hans.

"Holy St. Bavon!" exclaimed the dame, springing over the doorstep. "What ails the boy!"

"Come quick, mother," he cried. "Don't you see?

This is the spot—right here on the south side of the stump. Why didn't we think of it last night? The stump is the old willow-tree—the one you cut down last spring because it shaded the potatoes. That little tree wasn't here when father—Huzza!"

Dame Brinker could not speak. She dropped on her knees beside Hans just in time to see him drag forth the old stone pot! Yes, there was the long lost treasure!

Such a time! Such laughing! Such crying! Such counting, after they went into the cottage! And Dame Brinker and her children had a fine súpper, I can assure you. No need of saving the delicacies now.

"We'll get father some nice fresh things to-morrow," said the dame, as she brought forth cold meat, wine, bread and jelly, and placed them on the clean pine table. "Sit by, children, sit by."

That night, Annie fell asleep wondering whether it was a knife Hans had lost, and thinking how funny it would be if he should find it, after all.

Hans had scarce closed his eyes, before he found himself trudging through a thicket; pots of gold were lying all around, and watches, and skates, and glittering beads were swinging from every branch.

Strange to say, each tree, as he approached it, changed into a stump, and on the stump sat the prettiest fairy imaginable, clad in a scarlet jacket, and blue petticoat.

CHAPTER XXXIX

THE MYSTERIOUS WATCH

Something else than the missing guilders was brought to light on the day of the fairy godmother's visit. This was the story of the watch that for ten long years had been so jealously guarded by Raff's faithful vrouw. Through many an hour of sore temptation she had dreaded almost to look upon it, lest she might be tempted to disobey her husband's request. It had been hard to see her children hungry and to know that the watch if sold, would enable the roses to bloom in their cheeks again—"But nay," she would exclaim, "Meitje Brinker is not one to forget her man's last bidding, come what may."

"Take good care of this, mine vrouw," he had said, as he handed it to her—that was all.

Then one day Dame Brinker, with suppressed excitement, had laid the watch in her husband's hand. Brinker turned the bright, polished thing over and over in his hand; he seemed hardly to recognize it. At last he said, "Ah, I remember this! Why, you've been rubbing it, vrouw, till it shines like a new guilder."

Raff looked at it again. "Poor boy!" he murmured, then fell into a brown study.

Dame Brinker's curiosity was too strong for her. "Is the man—the lad—thou wert talking of dead, think ye?"

"It's hard telling," he answered.

"Was he so sick, Raff?"

"No, not sick, I may say; but troubled."

"Was it a crime, Raff?" whispered the wife, not daring to look up.

"Aye, Meitje, like to murder; that he told me him-

self. But I'll never believe it. He was a likely lad,
fresh and honest looking as our own youngster. He
came upon me quite sudden, I had never seen his
face before, the palest, frightenest face that ever was.
He caught me by the arm. 'You are an honest man,'
he says. 'Take me down the river a way. It is an
affair of life and death.' There was a boat close by,
and I took him down, it might be six or eight miles,
and then he said he could run the rest of the way on
shore. I was in haste to get the boat back. Before
he jumped out, he says, sobbing-like, 'I can trust you.
I've done a thing—God knows I never intended it—
but the man is dead. I must fly from Holland.' He
was dressed soft and fine as the prince himself. The
watch was his own, clear enough."

"How came he to give it up?" asked the dame.

"Well, just before jumping from the boat, he says,
handing me the watch, 'I'm flying from my country
as I never thought I could. I'll trust you because you
look honest. Will you take this to my father—not to-
day, but in a week, and tell him his unhappy boy sent
it; and tell him if ever the time comes that he wants
me to come back to him, I'll brave everything and
come. And tell him to send a letter to—to—' And
now it's all slipped me, and I've never seen the father
to this day."

"If you could remember that man's name, Raff,"
said his wife cautiously, "I might take the watch to
him, while you're sleeping. Could it be Boomphoffen?
I've heard how they've had two sons turn out bad—
Gerald and Lambert."

"It might be," said Raff. "Look if there's letters
on the watch; that'll guide us some."

"Bless thee, man," cried the dame, "why thou'rt
sharper than ever! Sure enough. Here's letters!
L.J.B. That's Lambert Boomphoffen you may de-

pend, though what the J is for I can't say. But the whole brood of them's been gone to America these four years. And now Raff, go to sleep. It'll all come to you, what's best to do, in the morning."

Before Raff awoke that evening, the fairy godmother, as we know, had been at the cottage, the guilders were once more safely locked in the big chest, and Dame Brinker and the children were faring sumptuously on meat and white bread and wine.

So the mother, in the joy of her heart, told them the story of the watch as far as she deemed it prudent to divulge it. It was no more than fair, she thought that the poor things should know, after keeping the secret so safe, ever since they had been old enough to know anything.

CHAPTER XL

A DISCOVERY

The next sun brought a busy day to the Brinkers.

In the first place the news of the thousand guilders had of course to be told to the father. Such tidings as that surely could not harm him. Then while Gretel was diligently obeying her mother's injunction to "clean the place fresh as a new brewing," Hans and the dame sallied forth to revel in the purchasing of peat and provisions.

"Can you call to mind, vrouw," said Raff, when his wife had returned, "the wonderful music-box that cheered your working in the big house at Heidelberg?"

"Aye, that I can," answered the dame, "I remember it well—but Raff, you would never throw our guilders away for a thing like that?"

"No, not I, vrouw—for the good Lord has already given me a music-box without pay. Ask Gretel, ask my little music-box, if your man has lacked comfort and joy this day."

"Not he, mother," laughed Gretel. "He's been my music-box, too. We sang together half the time you were gone."

After dinner, the affair of the watch was talked over, and the mysterious initials discussed. While they were still talking of this, there was a knock at the door, and Dr. Boekman came in. He was evidently in haste.

"Ahem!" he exclaimed, "not needed here, I perceive. The patient is mending fast."

"Well he may, mynheer," cried the dame, "for only last night we found a thousand guilders that's been lost to us these ten years."

"And now, mynheer," added Raff, "you can have your rightful pay; God knows you have earned it."

"Tut! tut!" said the doctor kindly, "say nothing about money. That boy's 'thank you'," nodding towards Hans, "was pay enough for me."

"Like enough ye have a boy of your own," said Dame Brinker, quite delighted to see the great man becoming so sociable.

Dr. Boekman made no actual reply; but his good natured smile vanished at once.

"Do not think the vrouw meddlesome, mynheer," said Raff, "she has been sore touched of late about a lad whose folks have gone away, none know where, and I had a message for them from the young gentleman."

"The name was Boomphoffen," said the dame eagerly, "and if he could get the watch to them with the poor lad's message it would be a most blessed thing. They had a son Lambert, and there's an L for Lambert and a B for Boomphoffen on the back; though to be sure there's an odd J too, but the meester can look for himself."

So saying, she brought forth the watch.

"L.J.B.!" cried Dr. Boekman, springing towards her.

Why attempt to describe the scene that followed? I need only say that the lad's message was delivered to his father at last—delivered while the great surgeon was sobbing like a little child.

"Laurens! my Laurens!" he cried, gazing tenderly at the watch. "Ah, if I had but known sooner! Laurens a homeless wanderer! Think, man, where is he? Where did my boy say the letter must be sent?"

"It's all gone, mynheer," said Raff sadly.

Hans, forgetting distinction of rank and station, threw his arms about the doctor's neck.

"I can find your son, mynheer. If alive, he is some-where, and I will devote every day of my life to the search. You are rich, mynheer, send me where you will."

"Yes, I am sure he is alive," cried the doctor. "You shall hear his story. Laurens acted as my assistant. By mistake he portioned out the wrong medicine for one of my patients—a deadly poison—but it was never administered, for I discovered the error in time. The man, however, died that day. I was de-tained with other cases until the next evening. When I reached home, my boy was gone. Poor Laurens!" sobbed the doctor, breaking down completely, "never to hear from me through all these years. His mes-sage disregarded. Oh, what must he have suffered!" Then he added more quietly, "I never dreamed, Brinker, that the boy had discovered the mistake. I believed it was youthful folly—ingratitude—love of adventure, that sent him away. My poor, poor Laurens!"

"But you know all, now, mynheer," whispered Hans. "You know he was innocent of wrong and that he loved you. We will find him. You shall see him again, dear meester."

"God bless you!" said Dr. Boekman, "it may be as you say. And Brinker, if ever the faintest gleam of recollection concerning him should come to you, you will send me word at once?"

"Indeed we will!" cried all but Hans, whose silent promise would have satisfied the doctor even had the others not spoken.

Then taking his son's watch, he said, "And now I must be gone. No medicine is needed by my patient; only peace and cheerfulness, and both are here in plenty. Heaven bless you, my good friends! I shall be ever grateful to you."

Hans went to the door with the doctor.

"When I can serve you, mynheer, I am ready."

"Very well, boy," replied Dr. Boekman with peculiar mildness. "Tell them, within, to say nothing of what has just passed. Meantime, Hans, when you are with your father, watch his mood. You have tact. At any moment he may suddenly be able to tell us more."

"Trust me for that, mynheer."

"Good-day, my boy!" cried the doctor, as he sprang into his stately coach.

"Aha!" thought Hans, as it rolled away, "the meester has more life in him than I thought."

CHAPTER XLI

THE RACE

The Twentieth of December came at last, bringing with it the perfection of Winter weather. All over the level landscape lay the warm sunlight. It tried its power on lake, canal and river; but the ice flashed defiance and showed no sign of melting. The very weather-cocks stood still to enjoy the sight. This gave the windmills a holiday. Nearly all the past week they had been whirling briskly; now, being rather out of breath, they rocked lazily in the clear, still air. Catch a windmill working when the weather-cocks have nothing to do!

There was an end to grinding, crushing, and sawing for that day. It was a good thing for the millers near Broek, who had early concluded anyway to take in their sails and go to the race.

The site selected was a faultless plain of ice near Amsterdam, on that great arm of the Zeider Zee which Dutchmen call the Eye. Everybody turned out— young and old, rich and poor, city people and country folk, natives and foreigners. And many of them were quaint in their costumes, some of which were so elaborate as to be worth many, many guilders.

Among the vast throngs of spectators, there are some familiar faces. High up in the centre of the great pavilion is Madame van Gleck. It is her birthday, you remember; she has the post of honor. There also is Mynheer van Gleck whose meerschaum has not really grown fast to his lips—it only appears so.

Near by, in another pavilion, sit the Van Holps with their son and daughter (the Van Gends) from The Hague. Peter's sister is not one to forget her promises. She has brought bouquets of exquisite hot-house flowers for the winners.

These pavilions, and there are others besides, have all been erected since daylight. That semicircular one, containing Mynheer Korbes' family, is very pretty; and the one with the blue flags is for the musicians. Those pagoda-like affairs, decked with sea-shells and streamers, are the judges' stands, and those columns and flag-staffs upon the ice mark the limits of the race-course. The two white columns twined with green form the starting point; and those flagstaffs, half a mile off, stand at each end of the boundary line, or turning point for the racers.

The racers themselves are all assembled together near the white columns. It is a beautiful sight—forty boys and girls in picturesque attire waiting for the contest.

Among them are some familiar faces. Lambert, Ludwig, Peter, and Carl are all there, cool and ready. Hans is not far off. Evidently he is going to join the race, for his skates are on—the very pair that he sold for seven guilders! He had soon suspected that his fairy godmother was the mysterious "friend" who bought them, and, having charged her with the deed, had now bought them back.

The twenty girls—Hilda, Rychie, Katrinka, Annie Bouman, Janzoon Kolp's sister, and Gretel (in a red jacket and a new grey petticoat) are among them— are in line now and ready to race. The music has ceased.

A man, whom we shall call the Crier, stands between the columns and the first judges' stand. He reads the rules in a loud voice:

"The girls and boys are to race in turn, until one girl and one boy has won twice. They are to go to the flagstaff line and back, thus making a mile at each run."

A flag is waved from the judges' stand. Madame van Gleck rises in her pavilion with a white handkerchief in her hand. When she drops it, a bugler will give the signal for the racers to start.

The handkerchief flutters to the ground. The bugle blows. They are off!

The racers speed down the course; and now they come flying back from the boundary mark. At first Katrinka is ahead; then Hilda. But before the columns are reached, Gretel, a flash of red and gray, shoots ahead. The judges lean forward. Cheer after cheer fills the air. Gretel has passed them all! Gretel has won!

While the girls are resting the boys form a line. Mynheer van Gleck drops the handkerchief this time. The bugles sound. And the boys have started!

Three hundred legs flash by in an instant—at least it seems like three hundred legs. Quickly the boys reach the half-mile mark, and begin the fight down the home stretch. And it is a great battle—between Hans and Peter. Close to the finish they are still ahead. But then young Schummel, gathering his powers at the last instant, whizzes between them, and passes the goal.

"Carl Schummel! One mile!" shouts the crier.

The girls now race again; and this time Hilda van Gleck, with the speed of an arrow, reaches the goal first. The final winner is still uncertain.

And with the boys, too, the result is still uncertain. In the second race Carl is badly beaten; and Peter, after a great struggle with Hans, wins.

Now the girls race for the third time—the time that may decide the winner. After a few moments they are speeding again towards the white columns.

Who is first? Not Rychie, Katrinka, Annie, Hilda, nor the girl in yellow—but Gretel—Gretel, the fleetest sprite of a girl that ever skated. The lithe form makes no apparent effort; but it cannot stop—not until the goal is passed!

In vain the crier lifts his voice—he cannot be heard. He has no news to tell—it is already ringing through the crowd. Gretel has won the Silver Skates!

With natural pride Hans turns to see if Peter van Holp is witnessing his sister's triumph. But Peter is kneeling, with a troubled face, and working hastily at his skate-strap. Hans is beside him at once.

"Are you in trouble, mynheer?"

"Ah, Hans! Yes, my fun is over. I tried to tighten the strap—to make a new hole—and this botheration of a knife has cut it nearly in two."

"Mynheer," pleads Hans in a husky voice, "you have called me your friend. Take this strap—quick! There is not an instant to lose. I shall not skate this time—indeed, I am out of practice. Mynheer, you must take it,"—and Hans, blind and deaf to any remonstrance, slips his strap into Peter's skate and implores him to put it on.

"Come, Peter!" cries Lambert from the line, "we are waiting for you."

"For madame's sake," pleads Hans, "be quick. She is motioning you to join the racers. There, the skate is almost on; quick, mynheer, fasten it. I could not possibly win. The race lies between Master Schummel and yourself."

"You are a noble fellow, Hans!" cries Peter, springing to his post just as the bugle sounds.

Off go the boys! And they all are hunting Peter van Holp.

The chase turns, and the skaters are coming this way. And Peter still leads. Fly, Peter—Hans is watching you, he is sending all his fleetness into your feet. Your mother and sister are pale with eagerness.

Hilda does not dare look up. Fly, Peter! The pursuers are close upon you! Touch the white column! It beckons—it is reeling before you—it—

Huzza! Huzza! Peter has won the Silver Skates!

And now the racers, both boys and girls, advance until they stand in a double semi-circle before Madame van Gleck's pavilion. Peter and Gretel are in the center in front of the others. Madame van Gleck rises majestically. Gretel trembles, but feels that she must look at the beautiful lady. She cannot hear what is said, there is such a buzzing all around her. She is thinking that she ought to make a curtsy, when suddenly something so dazzling is placed in her hand that she gives a cry of joy.

Then she ventures to look about her. Peter, too, has something in his hand—"Oh! oh! how splendid!" she cries, and "oh! how splendid!" is echoed as far as people can see.

Meantime the silver skates flash in the sunshine, throwing dashes of light upon those two happy faces.

Mevrouw van Gend sends a little messenger with her bouquets. One for Hilda, one for Carl, and others for Peter and Gretel.

At sight of the flowers the Queen of the Skaters becomes uncontrollable. With a bright stare of gratitude she gathers skates and bouquets in her apron—hugs them to her bosom, and darts off to search for her father and mother in the scattering crowd.

CHAPTER XLII

JOY IN THE COTTAGE

Perhaps you were surprised to learn that Raff and his vrouw were at the skating-race; you would have been more so had you been with them on the evening of that merry 20th of December. To see the Brinker cottage standing sulkily alone on the frozen marsh, with its bulgy, rheumatic-looking walls, and its slouched hat of a roof pulled far over its eyes, one would never suspect that a lively scene was passing within. Without, nothing was left of the day but a low line of blaze at the horizon. A few venturesome clouds had already taken fire, and others, with their edges burning, were lost in the gathering smoke.

Within the room a huge peat fire upon the hearth sent flashes of harmless lightning at the somber walls. It played in turn upon the great leathern Bible, upon Gretel's closet-bed, the household things on their pegs, and the beautiful Silver Skates and the flowers upon the table. Dame Brinker's honest face shone in the changing light; Gretel and Hans were leaning against the fireplace, laughing merrily; and Raff Brinker was dancing!

Suddenly he had sprung from his seat, performed two or three flourishes very much like the climax of a Highland Fling, and catching his vrouw in his arms had fairly lifted her from the ground in his delight.

"Huzza!" he cried, "I have it! It's Thomas Higgs. That's the name! It came upon me like a flash. Write it down lad, write it down!"

Just then there was a knock at the door, and three boys, Peter van Holp, Lambert, and Ben, entered. As soon as they were seated, Peter explained that they were on their way to a lecture at Amsterdam, and had stopped to return Hans's strap.

"And by the way, Hans," said Peter, "my father is very much pleased with your work. He would like to have the south arbor ornamented also, but I told him you were going to school again."

"Aye!" put in Raff. "Hans must go to school at once—and Gretel as well—that is true."

"I am glad to hear you say so," responded Peter, "and glad to know that you are again a well man."

"Yes, young master, a well man, and able to work as steady as ever—thank God!"

While they talked, Hans was hastily writing something on the edge of a time-worn almanac that hung by the chimney-place.

"Aye, that's right lad, set it down. Figgs! Wiggs! Alack!" added Raff in dismay, "it's gone again!"

"All right, father," said Hans, "the name's down now in black and white, and maybe the rest will come to you. If we had the place as well, it would be complete!" Then, turning to Peter, he said in a low tone, "I have an important errand in town, mynheer, and if—"

"Wist!" exclaimed the Dame, "not to Amsterdam tonight, and you've owned your legs were aching under you. Nay, it'll be soon enough to go at early daylight."

"Daylight indeed!" echoed Raff, "that would never do. Nay, Meitje, he must go at this hour."

And Dame Brinker at last agreed.

Just then Peter drew a long strap from his pocket, and, in handing it back to Hans, somewhat embarrassed him by his thanks.

"Ah, mynheer," Hans said, "from the first I felt stiff and strange on my feet; I was well out of it so long as I had no chance of winning."

But Peter looked rather distressed.

"We may hold different opinions there. That part of the business troubles me. It is too late to mend it now, but it would be really a kindness to me if—"

The rest of Peter's speech was whispered. But Hans started back in dismay, and Peter stammered out something to the effect that he would keep them, since he won the race, but it was "all wrong."

Here Van Mounen coughed, as if to remind Peter that lecture-hour was approaching fast. At the same moment Ben laid something upon the table—the skate-case that Gretel had forgotten to get from Madame van Gleck in the excitement of the prize-giving.

The case itself was elegantly made of crimson morocco, ornamented with silver; and "For the Fleet-est" was written upon the cover in sparkling letters. It was lined with velvet, and in one corner was stamped the name and the address of the maker.

Gretel thanked the boys; then, being quite delighted and confused, and not knowing what else to do, lifted the case, carefully examining it in every part. "It's made by Mynheer Birmingham," she said after awhile, still blushing and holding it before her eyes.

"Birmingham!" replied Lambert van Mounen. "That's the name of a place in England. Let me see it."

He looked for a moment, then said, "The case was made at Birmingham, but the maker's name is in smaller letters. Humph! they're so small, I can't read them."

"Let me try," said Peter, leaning over his shoulder. "Why man, it's perfectly distinct. It's—T—H—it's Thomas Higgs, to be sure."

As he said this he looked around in amazement. What was the matter with these people? Raff and

Hans had started up, and were staring at him in glad amazement. Gretel looked wild. Dame Brinker was rushing about the room crying, "Hans! Hans! where's your hat? Oh, the meester! the meester!"

"Good-night, mynheer," panted Hans, radiant with joy, "good-night—you will excuse me, I must go. Birmingham—Higgs—Higgs—Birmingham," and seizing his hat from his mother, and his skates from Gretel, he rushed from the cottage.

"You see, young masters," said Raff, "this Thomas Higgs is a person—a friend. We thought him dead. I hope it is the same man."

"I know the man," said Ben, addressing Lambert. "His factory is not four miles from our place—a queer fellow—doesn't seem at all like an Englishman. He made a beautiful writing-case once for me to give Jenny on her birthday."

As this was said in English, Van Mounen translated it for the benefit of the others, noticing meanwhile that neither Raff nor his vrouw looked very miserable, though Raff was trembling and the dame's eyes were swimming with tears.

You may believe the doctor heard every word of the story when later in the evening he came driving back with Hans. But Raff suggested that it would be a good idea for the doctor to see the "young English gentleman" before he had forgotten all about Thomas Higgs. And Dame Brinker added:

"You'll pick out the lad quick enough, mynheer, because he's in company with Master Peter van Holp; and his hair curls all up over his forehead like foreign folks' and, if you hear him speak, he talks kind of big and fast, only it's English; but that wouldn't be any hindrance to your honour."

The doctor had already lifted his hat to go. With a beaming face, he muttered something about its being just like the young scamp to give himself a rascally English name; called Hans "my son"—thereby making that young gentleman happy as a lord—and left the cottage with very little ceremony, considering what a great meester he was.

The grumbling coachman comforted himself by speaking his mind, as he drove back to Amsterdam. Since the doctor was safely stowed away in the coach and could not hear a word, it was a fine time to say terrible things of folks who hadn't no manner of feeling for nobody, and who were always wanting the horses a dozen times of a night.

CHAPTER XLIII

MYSTERIOUS DISAPPEARANCE OF THOMAS HIGGS

Higgs' factory was a mine of delight for the gossips of Birmingham. It was a small building, but quite large enough to hold a mystery. Who the proprietor was, or where he came from, none could tell. He looked like a gentleman—that was certain—though everybody knew he had risen from an apprenticeship; and he could handle his pen like a writing-master.

Years ago he had suddenly appeared in the place a lad of eighteen—learned his trade faithfully, and risen in the confidence of his employer—been taken in as a partner soon after his time was up—and, finally, when old Willett died, had assumed the business on his own hands. This was all that was known of his affairs.

His nationality was a great puzzle. The English name spoke plainly enough for one side of his house, but of what nation was his mother? If she had been a German, he would have known the language, and he didn't; if French it would have come out in his speech. No—it was most likely that he was Dutch. And strangest of all, though the man always pricked up his ears when you talked of Holland, he didn't seem to know the first thing about the country when you put him to the point.

Picture, then, the unbounded curiosity among all the good people when it was announced by "somebody who ought to know" that the postman had that very morning handed Higgs a foreign-looking letter, and the man had "turned as white as the wall; rushed to his factory; talked a bit with one of the head workmen; and, without bidding a creature good-bye, was off bag and baggage before you could wink, ma'am."

Mistress Scrubbs, his landlady, was deeply afflicted by this sudden departure; and her dearest friend, Miss Scrumpkins, ran home to tell all about it. And, as everybody knew the Scrumpkinses, a shining gossamer of news was soon woven from one end of the street to the other.

An investigating committee met, that evening, at Mrs. Snigham's—sitting, in secret sessions, over her best china. Though invited only to a quiet "tea," the amount of judicial business they transacted on the occasion was prodigious. The biscuits were actually cold before the committee had a chance to eat anything. There was so much to talk over—and it was so important that it should be firmly established that each member had always been "certain sure that something extraordinary would be happening to that man yet," that it was near eight o'clock before Mrs. Snigham gave anybody a second cup.

CHAPTER XLIV

BROAD SUNSHINE

One snowy day in January, Laurens Boekman went with his father to pay his respects to the Brinker family.

Raff was resting, after the labors of the day; Gretel, having filled and lighted his pipe, was brushing every speck of ash from the hearth; the dame was spinning; and Hans, perched upon a stool by the window, was diligently studying his lessons—a peaceful, happy household whose main excitement during the past week had been the looking forward to this possible visit from Thomas Higgs.

The grand presentation actually over, Gretel found out that she was disappointed. She had looked forward to a tragic scene; and here was the gentleman who had come so near being a murderer sitting by the fire just as pleasant and natural as could be! To be sure, his voice had trembled slightly when he talked with her parents; but he had not lifted his hand toward Heaven, saying, "I hereby swear to be forever faithful to my home, my God, and my country!" which would have been only right and proper under the circumstances.

Raff, however, was perfectly satisfied. The message was delivered; Dr. Boekman had his son; and the poor lad had done nothing sinful after all. Meantime, Hans was wholly occupied in the thought of Thomas Higgs' happiness in being able to be the meester's assistant again; and Dame Brinker was looking at the silver watch that the doctor was wearing and wondering what he had done with the gold one he used to wear.

The light was shining full upon Dr. Boekman's face. How contented he looked! How much younger and brighter than formerly! He was laughing as he said to the father:

"Am I not a happy man, Raff Brinker? My son will sell out his factory this month, and open a warehouse in Amsterdam. I shall have all my spectacle cases for nothing."

Hans started from his reverie. "A warehouse, mynheer! and will Thomas Higgs—I mean—is your son not to be your assistant again?"

"Oh no, Laurens has had quite enough of that. He wishes to be a merchant."

Hans appeared so surprised and disappointed that his friend asked good-naturedly:

"Why so silent, boy? Is it any disgrace to be a merchant?"

"N—not a disgrace, mynheer," stammered Hans, "but—but the other calling is so much better, so much nobler."

The doctor regarded him sternly, and Hans felt the hot tears gathering under his lashes.

"It is an ugly business, boy, this surgery," said the doctor. "It requires great patience, self-denial, and perseverance."

"I am sure it does," cried Hans, kindling again. "It calls for wisdom, too, and a reverence for God's work. Ah, mynheer, it may have its drawbacks—but you do not mean what you say—it is great and noble, not ugly! Pardon me, mynheer. It is not for me to speak so boldly."

After this outburst the doctor said something quietly to Laurens. Then turning to Hans he abruptly asked him his age.

"Fifteen, mynheer," was the startled reply.

"Would you like to become a physician?"

"Yes, mynheer," answered Hans, quivering with excitement.

"Would you be willing to devote yourself to study, to go to the university—and, in time, be a student in my office?"

"Yes, mynheer."

"You would not grow restless, think you, and change your mind just as I had set my heart upon preparing you to be my successor?"

Hans' eyes flashed.

"No, mynheer, I would not change."

The doctor smiled. "Well, Hans, I see nothing to prevent us from carrying out this plan, if your father agrees."

"If the lad's inclined to study for a meester," said Raff, "it's all one to me. The money's all that's a-wanting, but it mightn't be long, with two strong pair of arms to earn it, before we—"

"Tut! tut!" interrupted the doctor, "if I take your right-hand man away, I must pay the cost, and glad enough will I be to do it. And Brinker," he continued, "my son Laurens will need a trusty, ready man like you when he opens his warehouse in Amsterdam; some one to overlook matters. Well—why don't you tell him yourself, you rascal?"

This last was addressed to the son, and did not sound half as fierce as it looks in print. The rascal and Raff soon understood each other perfectly.

"I'm loath to leave the dikes," said the latter, after they had talked together awhile, "but you have made me such a good offer, mynheer, I'd be robbing my family if I let it go past me."

Take a long look at Hans as he sits there staring gratefully at the meester, for you shall not see him again for many years.

And Gretel—Ah, what a vista of puzzling work suddenly opens before her! Yes, for dear Hans' sake she will study now. If he really is to be a meester, his sister must not shame his greatness.

How faithfully those glancing eyes shall yet seek for the jewels that lie hidden in rocky school-books! And how they shall yet brighten and droop at the coming of one who she knows of now, only as the boy who wore a red cap on that wonderful day when she found the Silver Skates in her apron!

But the doctor and Laurens are going. Dame Brinker is making her best curtsy. Raff stands beside her, looking every inch a man as he grasps the meester's hand. Through the open cottage door we can look out upon the level Dutch landscape all alive with the falling snow.

CHAPTER XLV

CONCLUSION

Our story is nearly told. Time passes in Holland just as surely and steadily as here; in that respect no country is odd.

To the Brinker family it has brought great changes. Hans has spent his years faithfully and profitably, conquering obstacles as they arose, and pursuing one object with all the energy of his nature. If often the way has been rugged, his resolution has never failed. Sometimes he echoes, with his good old friend, the words said long ago in that little cottage near Broek: "Surgery is an ugly business;" but always in his heart of hearts lingers the echo of those truer words, "It is great and noble! it awakes a reverence for God's work!"

Were you in Amsterdam to-day, you might see the famous Doctor Brinker riding in his grand coach to visit his patients; or, it might be, you would see him skating with his own boys and girls upon the frozen canal. For Annie Bouman, the beautiful, frank-hearted peasant girl, you would inquire in vain; but Annie Brinker, the vrouw of the great physician, is very like her—only, as Hans says, she is even lovelier, wiser, more like a fairy godmother than ever.

Peter van Holp also is a married man. I could have told you before that he and Hilda would join hands and glide through life together, just as years ago they skimmed side by side over the frozen, sunlit river.

At one time, I came near hinting that Katrinka and Carl would join hands. It is fortunate now that the report was not started, for Katrinka changed her mind, and is single to this day.

Rychie's soul has been stirred to its depths during these long years. Her history would tell how seed carelessly sown is sometimes reaped in anguish, and how a golden harvest may follow a painful planting. If I mistake not, you may be able to read the written record before long; that is, if you are familiar with the Dutch language. In the witty, but earnest author whose words are welcomed at this day, in thousands of Holland homes, few could recognize the haughty, flippant Rychie who scoffed at little Gretel.

Lambert van Mounen, and Ludwig van Holp, are good Christian men, and what is more easily to be seen at a glance, thriving citizens. Both are dwellers in Amsterdam, but one clings to the old city of that name, and the other is a pilgrim to the new. Van Mounen's present home is not far from Central Park, and he says if the New Yorkers do their duty, the Park will, in time, equal his beautiful Bosch, near the Hague. He often thinks of the Katrinka of his boyhood, but he is glad now that Katrinka, the woman, sent him away; though it seemed at the time his darkest hour. Ben's sister Jennie has made him very happy, happier than he could have been with any one else in the wide world.

Carl Schummel has had a hard life. His father met with reverses in business; and as Carl had not many warm friends, and above all, was not sustained by noble principles, he has been tossed about by Fortune's battledore until his gayest features are nearly all knocked off. He is a bookkeeper, in the thriving Amsterdam house of Boekman and Schimmelpenninck. Voostenwalbert, the junior partner, treats him kindly; and he, in turn, is very respectful to the "monkey with a long name for a tail."

Of all our group of Holland friends, Jacob Poot is the only one who has passed away. Good-natured, true-hearted and unselfish to the last, he is mourned now, as heartily as he was loved and laughed at while on earth. He grew to be very thin before he died, thinner than Benjamin Dobbs, who is now portliest among the portly.

Raff Brinker and his vrouw have been living comfortably in Amsterdam for many years—a faithful, happy pair; as simple and straight-forward in their good fortune as they were patient and trustful in darker days. They have a zommerhuis near the old cottage and thither they often repair with their children and grandchildren on the pleasant Summer afternoons when the pond-lilies rear their queenly heads above the water.

The story of Hans Brinker would be but half told if we did not leave him with Gretel standing near. Dear, quick, patient little Gretel! What is she now? Ask old Doctor Boekman, he will declare she is the finest singer, the loveliest woman in Amsterdam; ask Hans and Annie, they will assure you she is the dearest sister ever known; ask her husband, he will tell you she is the brightest, sweetest little wife in Holland; ask Dame Brinker and Raff, their eyes will glisten with joyous tears; ask the poor, the air will be filled with blessings.

But, lest you forget a tiny form trembling and sobbing on the mound before the Brinker cottage, ask the Van Glecks; they will never weary telling of the darling little girl who won The Silver Skates.

THE END